When his laughter faded and he looked at her again, Malak's eyes were gleaming bright and she was breathless.

And in more trouble that she wanted to admit, she knew.

"There is a certain liberty in having so few choices," he told her, almost sadly, and it felt like a cage closing, a lock turning. "This will all work out fine, Shona. One way or another."

"There's nothing to work out," she said fiercely. Desperately. "You need to turn around and go back where you came from. Now."

"I wish I could do that," Malak said in that same resigned sort of way, and oddly enough, she believed him. "But it is impossible."

"You can't—"

"Miles is the son of the king of Khalia," Malak said, and there was an implacable steel in that dark gaze and all through that body of his, lean and sculpted to a kind of perfection that spoke of actual fighting arts, brutal and intense, not a gym.

And she believed that, too, though she didn't want to. She believed that every part of him was powerful. Lethal. And that she was in over her head.

Again.

"Congratulations, Shona," he continued, all steel and dark promise. "That makes you my queen."

Bound to the Desert King

One scandalous royal family, four irresistible sheikhs!

The royal family of Khalia has always presented an image of duty and responsibility. But the brother they never knew existed has just stepped into the palace—and all their lives will change forever!

Adir was exiled to the desert, then brutally rejected—now he's back for vengeance!

Sheikh's Baby of Revenge by Tara Pammi

Zufar's bride of convenience has just been kidnapped—now the maid must take her place...

Sheikh's Pregnant Cinderella by Maya Blake

Galila has just told her family's secrets to a stranger—but he's king of a neighboring kingdom!

Sheikh's Princess of Convenience by Dani Collins

Malak is now heir to the throne—but a secret in his past is about to be uncovered...

Sheikh's Secret Love-Child by Caitlin Crews

Available Now!

Caitlin Crews

SHEIKH'S SECRET LOVE-CHILD

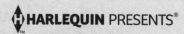 **HARLEQUIN** PRESENTS®

Recycling programs for this product may not exist in your area.

Special thanks and acknowledgment are given to Caitlin Crews for her contribution to the Bound to the Desert King series.

ISBN-13: 978-1-335-41983-5

Sheikh's Secret Love-Child

First North American publication 2018

Copyright © 2018 by Harlequin Books S.A.

Printed in U.S.A.

USA TODAY bestselling and RITA® Award–nominated author **Caitlin Crews** loves writing romance. She teaches her favorite romance novels in creative-writing classes at places like UCLA Extension's prestigious Writers' Program, where she finally gets to utilize the MA and PhD in English literature she received from the University of York in England. She currently lives in the Pacific Northwest with her very own hero and too many pets. Visit her at caitlincrews.com.

Visit the Author Profile page
at Harlequin.com for more titles.

CHAPTER ONE

WHEN THE OTHER shoe finally dropped, and hard, Shona Sinclair couldn't say she was entirely surprised.

Horrified, yes. Terrified—certainly.

But not surprised.

On some level, she had always known this day would come.

Get ready, she told herself stoutly. *Because it's finally here.*

There were four men, cold-eyed and burly. She had never seen royal guards before, not in real life, but she hadn't the slightest doubt that was exactly what they were. She knew it the moment she saw them. They came into the restaurant in a kind of rolling, lethal wave. They looked to the right and to the left, not looking for tables like everyone else who wandered in from the streets of the French Quarter, but more as if they were taking stock of every single person in the place.

If asked, Shona was certain they'd have an accu-

rate count of all the busboys as well as the few pa-
trons scattered amongst the tables who picked at their
down-market gumbo and rubbery beignets.

Shona knew who they were. *She knew.* And more,
she knew what their appearance meant. She could
feel it like a shuddering thing that wrapped around
her and shook her so hard she couldn't breathe for
a moment.

But she still held out hope. She caught her breath
and she *hoped.*

It could be a celebrity, she told herself. That happened with some regularity here in New Orleans,
even in a less than A-list place like this. But these
men didn't have that Hollywood look. They were too
serious, for one thing.

And they were looking directly at her, for another.

It was early yet. The dinner service had yet to really kick into gear and the restaurant was still fairly
empty. But this was the famous French Quarter in
New Orleans. It could fill up at any time and fre-
quently did, because *"laissez les bon temps rouler"*
knew no set mealtimes.

Shona prayed for a crowd. Fervently.

But when the door opened, it wasn't a gift from
any god Shona knew. Another man walked in,
flanked by two more guards, and that was it.

It was all over.

Her worst nightmare had come to pass.

Because she knew the man who stood there, adjusting the cuffs of his mind-numbingly expensive-looking suit with impatient little jerks, gazing around as if he found his surroundings deeply offensive. He took in the decor, which was aimed directly at the tourist trade with vintage New Orleans street signs and Saints football memorabilia plastering the walls.

Then he took his time redirecting that dark, arrogant gaze of his back to Shona.

Where it held.

And she knew too much about him. Things that crowded into her memory and flowed like a kind of painful lava all through her body no matter how she tried to tell herself he didn't affect her.

He did.

He still did.

She knew that his eyes were not black, as they seemed from a distance, but were instead a breathtaking dark green she had only ever seen on one other human being. And that his face was even more of a marvel up close, all high cheekbones and that hard, tempting mouth. And his hands, elegant and strong all at once, could work magic.

Shona knew that his laugh could make a woman forget herself completely and his smile could make that same woman think that losing herself like that was worth it.

She'd forgotten many things since that searing night five years ago—her sense of humor, maybe, and any sense of who that silly girl had been that night she'd changed her life forever thanks to her own foolishness and a gorgeous stranger in a bar—but she hadn't forgotten him.

Despite her best attempts.

"Hello, Shona," he said, and even his voice was the same. "How nice to see you again."

She had never forgotten the sound of him, either. That low, rich voice that washed over her like a caress, his cultured British accent layered with hints of his own country, the faraway kingdom of Khalia.

Shona had never heard of Khalia before she'd met him. And now she knew far more than she wanted about a place she had no intention of ever seeing firsthand. Such as where the kingdom was situated, tucked there on the Arabian Peninsula above the sparkling Arabian Sea. Its royal family. Its standing in the international community, even. She'd made it her business to know as much as possible ever since that terrible day five years ago, when she'd opened up a magazine in her obstetrician's office to discover that the baby she was carrying—the result of a one-night stand with a stranger whose name she didn't know in full and whom she'd assumed she'd never see again—belonged to Prince Malak of Khalia.

He had been right there on a glossy gossip magazine page, dripping in blonde supermodels in one of the many fancy European cities Shona had never visited and knew she never would. Places like Europe were little more than fantasies for a girl like Shona, who'd had no family, no prospects and a chip on her shoulder about both that she liked to think of as her own personal pet.

Princes were even more unattainable than trips to Europe, she was sure. She'd had absolutely no doubt that if she actually managed to reach him to tell him what had happened and that, surprise, he had a baby on the way—assuming a prince could be *reached* in the first place, because she doubted anyone could simply call the man at will—he would bluster back into her life the way men like him always seemed to do with women like her. He would do nothing but cause trouble, because that was what rich men did. Because they could. She'd seen it happen more than once. Women down on Shona's level were good for a night or two, maybe, but certainly not good enough to carry a rich man's child.

As far as Shona could tell, wealthy men seemed to travel with legal teams at the ready to draw up nondisclosure agreements and engineer payoffs at a moment's notice—anything to keep the baby far away from the man's real family and the wife who usually knew nothing about her husband's extracurricular activities. As well as curtail any future blackmail scenarios. But those were the happy stories. Far scarier were the women who'd lost their babies altogether because they didn't have the money to fight in court.

That wasn't going to happen to her, Shona had

vowed that day in the doctor's office, the glossy magazine wrinkling in her panicked grip. She had nothing in the world but her baby and she'd be keeping him, come hell, high water or some random royal sheikh.

Shona had never wanted to lay eyes on Prince Malak of Khalia again.

That hadn't changed.

"Do not pretend you do not remember me," Malak said, as Shona started to tell that very lie. That mouth of his curved, and she thought there was something sardonic in the way he looked at her across the sticky floor of the restaurant. "I can see that you do. And besides, lying is so unbecoming, is it not?"

Her body melted at the sound of his voice. In ways that she planned to beat out of herself when she'd handled this, by hand, if necessary. But in the meantime, he certainly didn't need to know that he still had that effect on her.

"I can't say I particularly care if you find anything I do becoming or not," Shona replied, the same way she would to any crazy person who wandered in off the streets. Her reward was instant expressions of outrage from his guards, though Malak's dark eyes only gleamed. "I see you've come with friends this time. A social call, I can only assume. Too bad I'm so busy or I'd love to catch up."

Malak smiled at that, though it was nothing like the smile she remembered from that night. This one was cool. Powerful, somehow. It made something deep inside her uncoil in a kind of white-hot panic. Worse, he didn't dismiss his guards, which told Shona all she needed to know about whether or not this was just a weird kind of coincidence years too late. A thick sort of uneasiness wound its way around and around her, until it felt like a noose pulled tight.

Because while it was always possible that he'd come back because he cycled through all his affairs every few years or so and conducted reunions as a matter of course, she knew that was highly unlikely. This was a famous prince, for God's sake. He was knee-deep in willing women wherever he went. Why would he need to repeat himself?

Which left exactly one reason he would be here in the restaurant where she worked, not at her home—likely, she thought in a sickening rush of understanding, because he'd already been to her little rental house on a not-great street a fifteen-minute walk from the French Quarter.

She was wildly, insanely happy she'd dropped Miles at her friend Ursula's house before work. Though perhaps *friend* was a strong word. Ursula had a six-year-old and also worked strange hours. They'd met years ago, waiting tables in the same place a few blocks over, and had been swapping child care ever since. They were bound together by necessity and the odd drink here and there, that was all.

The truth was, Shona knew as little about friendship as she did about family.

"Is there somewhere we can talk?" Malak asked.

And she hadn't known *him* more than that single, fateful night five years ago, it was true. But the man she'd thought he was during that long, impossibly carnal night that she refused to be ashamed of, no matter what had happened afterward, had never sounded like that.

As if he was not so much asking a question, but delivering orders.

And woe betide the person who did not obey them.

But Shona had never been very good at following orders. That was what came of growing up hard, the way she had. Her own mother had abandoned her to the state when she was a baby and she'd had nothing but indifferent foster care and what she liked to call *opportunities*, ever since.

Opportunities to learn how to be tough, no matter what came at her. Opportunities to figure out how to stand on her own two feet and take care of herself, because nobody else would. Or ever did.

She'd been eighteen when she'd been set free by the state at last. She'd made her own way ever since, before and after she'd found herself pregnant and yet again on her own.

And she wasn't about to change that for some uppity prince in a suit that almost certainly cost more than a year's rent.

"No," she told him. She could tell by the way he raised his brow that it wasn't a word he often heard. Or had ever heard, possibly. "There is no place we can talk."

"No?" Malak echoed, as if she might have said it by accident and would reverse herself once she heard it repeated back to her.

She didn't. "We have nothing to talk about."

Shona folded her arms over her chest and she was fiercely glad that she looked like exactly what she was today. She wasn't dressed up the way she had been when she'd met him that fateful night. She was a waitress, nothing more and nothing less, and she wasn't the least bit ashamed of that. She wore the restaurant's black T-shirt with the silly logo stamped on the front, a little black apron wrapped around her hips and the short red skirt the owner insisted upon, and Shona didn't mind too much, because it helped with tips. She had scraped her hair back from her face and let it do its own thing at the back, like a high, black cloud of tight curls.

Shona imagined she looked as far beneath the notice of a fancy prince from a far-off country as she was, and that was a good thing. Maybe it would remind Malak why he'd disappeared that morning five years before. Maybe, if she made sure to trumpet her obvious lack of breeding and class, he'd repeat his disappearing act.

She could only hope.

"I'm afraid that we have quite a few things to talk about," Malak said in that same way of his, that suggested he was speaking laws aloud, not having a conversation. There was something about it that clawed at her, making her feel a kind of restlessness she refused to acknowledge. "And there can be no avoiding it, much as you might wish otherwise."

As he spoke, he thrust his hands into the pockets of his trousers and shifted the way he stood. And then he smiled as if he had come here to do nothing but charm her.

And this, then, was the man that Shona remembered so vividly from that night five years ago, there in that hotel bar she'd always wanted to go to, when she was growing up. It had almost gotten lost in the elegant suit and the security detail, but she remembered that smile. How infectious it was. How sensual. And how it had spurred her on to act so completely out of character.

She had steadfastly refused to regret what had happened there, all this time. But now, with her heart a wild drumbeat in her chest and her breath tight and a little too close to being labored, she was afraid that everything had changed.

Because the Malak she remembered—lazy and wicked, boneless and seductive—wasn't a figment of her imagination, after all. He might look different now. He'd stood taller before and his mouth was far grimmer. He seemed less playful, less endlessly amused.

But it was still him, and when he stood more casually it was impossible to keep herself from remembering…everything.

And that was a big problem, because Shona had never reacted to any man the way she did to him. The truth was, she'd never touched any man but him.

She shoved aside that thought, because it was the least of her worries and really, something she ought to have done something about before now. Suddenly, all these years when she'd thought she was too tired, too stressed, too poor, too *something* to get out there and meet someone seemed like a character flaw, not simple self-protection. Because Shona hated the fact that Malak was the sum total of her experience of sex and men when he also had the power to ruin her life.

Again.

"Even if we had something to talk about, which we don't, I'm at work," she told him in the same tone she'd used before. As if the moment she could, she'd be dialing 911 to have him bodily removed and possibly subjected to a psychiatric evaluation. "This is neither the time nor the place for your goon squad or you. You should try calling, like a normal person."

"A call would not have sufficed in this situation."

"We have no situation," Shona said, with a little more force.

Because there was only one thing that he could possibly be talking about, and Shona was not going to let this happen. She would die first.

She'd worried about this moment for years. And now that it was here, it was as if she had done all her panicking already. Maybe that was why, despite the pounding of her heart and that sick feeling in her belly, she found herself focusing hard on Malak instead of giving in to all the sick feelings churning around inside of her. She noticed the way his guards had blocked all the exits. She calculated what she had to do to make it through this so she could run, pick up Miles from Ursula's and get the hell out of New Orleans.

The great thing about coming from nothing and having only slightly more than nothing to her name now was that disappearing would be no problem. She was barely on the grid as it was. All she had to do was get away from Malak tonight and she could go somewhere—anywhere—far away from here. It would be like she and Miles had never existed.

She was kicking herself for not doing exactly that five years ago.

"You are correct, of course," Malak said, a dangerous light in those eyes of his. Miles's eyes. "He is not a situation at all, is he? He's a little boy. I believe you call him Miles, do you not?"

She wasn't calm at all, Shona realized then. She was frozen solid, but not in fear. Or not only in fear. She was stitched through with fury, red and bright. "Miles is no concern of yours."

"Something you must believe very strongly indeed," he murmured, and there was something even harder about him then. It pricked at Shona like an accusation. "If you prefer to raise him in squalor rather than as what and who he is. The only son of a prince of Khalia."

"I don't know or care who his father is," Shona gritted out at him. "What matters is that he's mine."

"Let me tell you what happens when a prince becomes king," Malak told her, his voice soft with a different kind of menace. "No need to offer your condolences, as I am certain you were about to. Neither my father nor my brother died. They abdicated, one after the next, like royal dominos."

And Shona couldn't quite take that in. She didn't want to make sense of what he was telling her. Because that would mean…

But he was still talking. "Transfers of power are always fraught with peril, I am sure, but perhaps never more so than when the new king was never meant to come anywhere near the throne. First, the palace advisors rend their garments and pray for deliverance, of course. That takes some time. But when they are done, when reality has set in on all sides, they launch a full investigation into the new monarch, a man who…how shall I say this—?"

"Couldn't keep it in his pants?"

His mouth curved, though whether it was at her dry tone or because he actually found that description of himself amusing, she couldn't tell.

"As you may recall, Shona, nobody wanted me to keep it in my pants. Least of all you." He shrugged when her eyes narrowed at that. But it wasn't as if she could argue. He wasn't wrong. "The palace investigators had their hands full, I regret to say. They found every woman I've ever touched."

"I wouldn't think anyone could count that high."

Malak inclined his head, but that gaze of his never left hers. And she was beginning to imagine it might leave marks. "Each lucky paramour was thoroughly investigated to make certain there was nothing about her or her liaison with me that could embarrass the kingdom. And of them all, Shona, this great and glorious legion of former lovers, only you were keeping the kind of secret that makes the average palace aide turn gray overnight."

"You are mistaken." She was gripping herself too hard. But she didn't let up, even though she was half afraid she would crush her own ribs with her crossed arms. "Miles and I have nothing to do with you."

"I admire your independence," he told her in a tone that suggested the opposite. "I do. But I'm afraid there are no choices here. Or, I should say, none I expect you will like. The boy is mine. That makes him the heir to the Khalian throne. And that means he cannot stay here."

She dug her fingers into her sides, but she didn't wake up. This was a nightmare she'd had more than once since she'd given birth to Miles, but this time, she couldn't jolt herself awake. She couldn't make Malak go away.

"Let me make sure that you understand something," Shona said, though there was a ringing in her ears. Her heart still pounded, but it had gone slow. Intense. And she was focused on Malak as if he was a target, if only she could find the right weapon. "You will not touch my child and if you try, six beefed-up goons with guns won't save you. Nothing will."

She didn't know what she expected Malak to do then.

But it wasn't the way he threw back his head and laughed, with all that infectious delight and lazy sensuality that had been her downfall five years ago. His laughter had not changed at all. The dark and somber suit was new, as were the guards surrounding him. That grave note in his voice, this talk of kings and thrones and palace advisors—all of that was new, too.

But that laugh… It was as dangerous as she remembered it.

More, maybe, because unlike back then, it was wholly unwelcome.

It curled into her like smoke. It wound through her, insinuating itself into every crevice and beneath every square inch of her skin. It licked into her like heat, and then worse, wound itself into a kind of fist between her legs. Then pulsed.

She'd told herself she'd been drunk that night.

She'd told herself she'd imagined that pull she'd felt when she was near him, that irresistible urge to get closer no matter what. That aching, restless thing inside her that hummed for him only. She'd imagined all of that, she'd been so sure—because she'd never felt it again. She'd never felt anything the slightest bit like it, not with any man who'd come near her before or since.

But she hadn't imagined it.

It turned out that he was the only man in the entire world who made her feel all those things. And if anything, she'd let time and memory mute his potency.

He was standing here with armed guards, threatening her baby and life as she knew it, and that didn't keep her from feeling it. What the hell was the matter with her?

When his laughter faded and he looked at her again, Malak's eyes were gleaming bright and she was breathless.

And in more trouble that she wanted to admit, she knew.

"There is a certain liberty in having so few choices," he told her, almost sadly, and it felt like a cage closing, a lock turning. "This will all work out fine, Shona. One way or another."

"There's nothing to work out," she said fiercely. Desperately. "You need to turn around and go back where you came from. Now."

"I wish I could do that," Malak said in that same

resigned sort of way, and oddly enough, she believed him. "But it is impossible."

"You can't—"

"Miles is the son of the king of Khalia," Malak said, and there was an implacable steel in that dark gaze and all through that body of his, lean and sculpted to a kind of perfection that spoke of actual fighting arts, brutal and intense, and not a gym.

And she believed that, too, though she didn't want to. She believed that every part of him was powerful. Lethal. And that she was in over her head.

Again.

"Congratulations, Shona," he continued, all steel and dark promise. "That makes you my queen."

CHAPTER TWO

MALAK WAS FURIOUS.

That was too tame a word. He was nearly volcanic, and the worst part was, he was well aware he had no right to the feeling because he'd been the one to cause this situation in the first place. No one had asked him to carry on as he had, following pleasure wherever it led.

But knowing his own culpability only made it worse.

He hadn't believed it when the palace advisors had put the photographs before him. He'd had enough on his plate, with his brother Zufar's abdication following so soon after their father's and the bracing news that after a life of being ignored—which he had always quite enjoyed, in fact, as it had meant he could do exactly as he pleased without anyone thundering at him about his responsibilities—he was to be king.

Malak had never wanted to be king. Who would *want* such a burden? He'd preferred his life of excess and extremes, thank you. But Zufar was happy, a thing that Malak would never have believed possible if he hadn't seen it with his own eyes, not after the way they'd grown up. And Malak loved both his brother and his country, so the decision was simple.

The decision, perhaps, but not the execution of it. His initiation into his new role had thus far been all that he'd feared and more, starting with a close examination of his entire sybaritic existence. Laying all his exploits bare, one by one, until Malak was profoundly sick of himself and the great many salacious, debauched urges he'd never attempted to curb in the slightest.

He had never been much for shame, but it was difficult to avoid when faced with *so many* photographs and *so many* thick dossiers enumerating his indiscretions, one after the next, on into infinity. And particularly when so many of the women in those pages were nothing but vaguely pleasant blurs to him.

And yet he remembered Shona. Distinctly.

How could he not? Of the many beautiful women he'd been privileged enough to sample, she had been something else entirely. It had been his last night in New Orleans after a week of blues and all manner of questionable behavior. He had settled in for a quiet drink in the lobby of his quietly elegant hotel to prepare himself for the trip back home to see his family, who would all have been deeply disapproving of his antics if they'd ever spared him a moment's notice.

And then there she was. She'd been almost unbearably pretty, with rich, creamy dark skin and a lush mouth that made him feel distinctly greedy at a glance. And her beautiful hair, arrayed in a great halo around her head with springy curls he'd longed to sink his hands into. She'd worn a skimpy little dress that had glittered like gold and had made a delectable poem out of her lean curves.

Better still, she'd walked to the gleaming wooden bar and taken the only empty seat, which had been directly next to his.

Malak was only a man. And not much of one, according to his family when they bothered to pay attention to him and all the newspapers that breathlessly recorded his every salacious move.

Which had made it the easiest thing in the world to smile at the prettiest girl he'd seen in ages, and lean in when she smiled back with what had seemed to him, as jaded as he was, like innocence.

It had been a revelation.

"This is my first time here," she'd told him, angling her head toward his as if she was sharing a secret. "Tonight is my twenty-first birthday and I decided to celebrate in style."

It had taken him a minute to remember where he was. And more, recall those American laws he found so strange, that called young boys and girls adults when they were eighteen and wished to head off to war, but restricted their drink.

"And you chose to celebrate it here?" he'd asked. "Surely there are more exciting places to go for such a grand occasion than a subdued hotel bar on a quiet street. This is New Orleans, after all."

Her smile had only gotten better the longer she'd aimed it at him. "I used to walk past this hotel all the time when I was a kid and I always dreamed I'd come in here one day. This seemed like the perfect opportunity."

Malak had known full well that he hadn't been alone when he'd felt that spark between them. That fire.

It had never occurred to him to ignore such things back then, for some notion of a greater good. He hadn't. He'd bought a pretty girl her first drink and then he'd happily divested her of her innocence in his suite upstairs. He could remember her wonder, her uncomplicated joy, as easily as if it had all happened yesterday.

Just as he was sure that if he tried, he would be able to remember her taste, too.

Because it wasn't only Shona's smile that had been a revelation to him.

The pictures his advisors had shown him—his aides bristling with officious dismay as they'd set each one before him—were of the only woman he remembered in such perfect detail. He knew time had passed—years, in fact—but he wouldn't have known that by looking at the photographs they'd placed before him. Shona was as pretty as ever, whether she wore what appeared to be a server's uniform or one of those long, flowing sundresses she seemed to prefer that Malak greatly approved of, so perfectly did they showcase those curves he could almost feel beneath his hands again.

Or perhaps she was even prettier because he found he could also remember the wild sounds of wonder and discovery she'd made as he'd explored her, and the sumptuous feel of her silky dark skin against his.

But his advisors had not been primarily interested in reacquainting Malak with his every mistake. Those forced marches down memory lane had become tense for all concerned, since Malak had resolutely refused to apologize or show the faintest shred of regret for the way he'd lived his life as the spare with no hope of ascending the throne. Ever.

It was the child his advisors were interested in.

The child, who was four years old and bore a striking resemblance not only to Malak, but also to every member of his family. And if there had been any doubt, the little boy sported the same dark green eyes that had been a gift from Malak's great-grandmother. The same damn eyes Malak saw every time he looked at his reflection.

And he had never expected to be king, it was true. He'd never wanted such a burden. But he was a prince of Khalia whether his distant father ignored him while campaigning for his mother's affections, or his mother ignored him because she'd preferred the son Malak had only recently learned she'd had and given away after falling in love with another man. Royal blood ran in his veins and despite his many heedless years of living down to everybody's worst expectations of him, Malak had agreed to do his duty and was fully prepared to acquit himself well.

Without the issues that had plagued his parents, thank you, since Malak had no intention of ruining himself for love the way they each had, in their way.

He was getting his head around the constant surveillance, whether from his own security detail or the public that had always wanted a piece of him and now wanted *everything*. He was getting up to speed on current affairs and was learning to pick his way between competing agendas to find his own opinion on matters of state.

He was no one's first choice to be king—he recognized that. But that didn't mean he wouldn't do his best to be a good one.

And that meant that Malak did not have to be told what it meant that a one-night affair had borne such fruit. Not that this spared him numerous lectures on the topic from his affronted advisors, as if, left to his own devices, he would simply ignore the fact that he had a child out there in the world he'd never met.

He knew what it meant. And he was furious that Shona had concealed his son from him—even though he was fairly certain he hadn't told her who he really was. That didn't change the fact that he had missed years of his own child's life.

Or that he was now trapped in a mess of his own making.

A mess that would have to become a marriage, regardless of any feelings he might have on the matter.

Furious barely began to cover his feelings on the topic, no matter how pretty Shona still was or how sweetly she'd surrendered her innocence to him all those years ago. There was not one part of Malak that wanted to marry a woman he hardly knew, or any woman at all if he was honest, simply because he'd clearly made a very big mistake five years back.

But it turned out he liked *her* horror at the same idea even less.

"I hope you mean your 'queen' in a metaphoric sense," she snapped at him in obvious outrage, as if he'd suggested she prostitute herself on the nearest corner. Her arms were crossed, as if she was trying to ward off one of the many disreputable persons he'd had to step over on the street outside.

As if *he* was one of said disreputable persons.

New Orleans, it turned out, was a very different city in the light. And while sober.

And perhaps Shona was, too.

He studied her a moment while he fought to keep his temper in check. "You will find I rarely traffic in metaphors."

"I don't care." She shook her head at him, very much as if he was insane. "What you do or don't do is of no interest to me. You need to leave, now, or I'm calling the police. And believe me when I tell you that I'm not into metaphors, either."

She pulled her mobile from the pocket of her apron and Malak believed her. If there was a woman alive on this earth who would dare summon the local police to attempt to handle him, it would be this one.

Shona was fierce, it turned out, and his was the blood of desert kings. Fierceness was appreciated—or it would be, eventually, if he could focus it in the right direction. She was threatening him, as if she had no fear at all of the armed men who would die to protect him, and he could appreciate that, too. Theoretically.

But the truth was, he wasn't at all certain that an American waitress of questionable finances and a "career" in restaurants like this depressing, grotty pit should find the idea of marrying the king of Khalia *quite* so appalling.

What he found he was certain of was that he didn't like it.

"I invite you to call all the police you imagine will help you," he told her, and he could hear that volcanic rage in his voice, humming just there beneath the surface. The faint widening of her perfect brown eyes told him she could, too. "I'm sure they will enjoy a lesson in diplomatic immunity as much as they'll enjoy discussions with you about wasting their time. But the end result will not change. Perhaps it is time you considered accepting the inevitable."

She made an alternate, anatomically impossible suggestion that made Malak's entire security team bristle to outraged attention.

"The disrespect, sire!" the man on his right growled.

Malak merely held up a hand, and his men subsided. Because no one was getting the fight they wanted today.

"I would advise you to remember that, like it or not, I am a king," he told her softly. "It is possible I might find this irrepressible spirit of yours intriguing, in time, but my men most assuredly will not."

She let out a short laugh that was almost as offensive as the off-color suggestion she'd just made. "The only thing I care about less than you is the opinion of your babysitters."

Malak did not respond to that bit of impudence the way he wanted to do.

Because this was not Khalia. This was America, where, diplomatic immunity or not, people would likely take a dim view of him tossing a screaming woman over his shoulder and then throwing her into his waiting car.

Besides, that was no kind of strategy. Allowing her to think she could speak to him in this way was setting a dangerous precedent, but he could handle disrespect. He could think of several enjoyable ways to do just that even as he stood here in this distressingly dank hole that called itself a restaurant, the last place on earth he would ordinarily find himself feeling so...needy.

But he didn't want to kidnap Shona and his own son. He would certainly do it if it came to that, but he knew that would do nothing but make him her enemy. Neither one of them wanted this unavoidable connection and the marriage that had to follow, that was plain enough, but it would be far better for him if she surrendered to the inevitable rather than fought him every step of the way.

At the very least it would be better for his relationship with the small child he had yet to meet whom he'd helped create—a notion he still couldn't entirely get his head around.

After all, he knew more than he needed to know about what it was like to grow up in the shadow of a terrible marriage. He had no intention of passing on that feeling to his own child—even one he'd only learned existed a week ago.

"I will wait for you outside," he said, with great magnanimity, as if he was bestowing upon her a tremendous favor. It made her eyes narrow. And then he could *see* the thoughts that spun through her head, so he addressed them. "My men are already at every exit, Shona, so escape is out of the question. What you need to ask yourself is if you want me to pay your boss to fire you, too. Simply because I can. With ease. And because it would suit me to speed up this process."

"Of course you'd threaten me with losing my livelihood," she replied, shaking her head at him as if he disgusted her. He found he did not enjoy the sensation. "After all, what's a job to you? You don't have to put food on any tables. You probably think it all just appears there, like magic."

Malak did not dignify that with a response. He turned on his heel and went outside instead, where night was beginning to creep into the French Quarter, and as it did, as the soupy heat of the day began to ebb.

Outside in the thick, sweet twilight he could wrestle with his temper before he caused an international incident. Something that would not bother *him* in the slightest, he felt certain, because it would get him what he wanted that much quicker—but would cause the people of Khalia more alarm. And his people had been through enough already in these last few turbulent months.

He expected her to follow after him directly, but she didn't. She made him wait. She not only did not walk away from her job as he expected she might, but she also worked her entire shift. And on her breaks she tested every single exit he'd told her he was having watched, which his men dutifully reported to him each time.

Malak almost admired her thoroughness and commitment.

Almost.

When she finally walked out of the restaurant and saw him waiting for her as he'd told her he would, she tilted up that belligerent little chin of hers and fixed him with the same scowl she'd used inside.

It took a great deal more self-control than it should have not to object to that…in a manner that involved his hands on her and the horizontal back seat of his vehicle. Malak complimented himself on his own restraint, because he very much doubted Shona would.

"I don't know what you think is going to happen," she began, her tone hot.

"I have already told you what's going to happen." Malak leaned against the pristine side of the Range Rover his security detail had driven here from the private airfield where his jet waited. The New Orleans night was sultry, just as he recalled it. There had been people around in the daylight, but they seemed wilder and brighter in the dark. Their laughter spiced the air as they wandered down the street and followed the seductive sound of the music that snaked around every corner.

In the middle of it, he and Shona stood there, studying each other with mutual dislike.

You do not dislike her, a voice inside challenged him at once. *You dislike the fact she dislikes you, and so openly.*

He opted to ignore that. He was unused to being disliked. Ignored or desired, that was what Malak was familiar with. But never this…hatred.

"I am not going to be your queen," she told him, very distinctly. "I'm willing to let you see Miles, because, like it or not, you're his father, And he deserves to know you, I suppose."

He stopped admiring his restraint and forced himself to use it. "You suppose."

"All you are to me is a man in a bar," Shona said quietly, her dark gaze on his. And there was no reason that should have slammed into Malak like a blow when it was no more than the truth. "I don't want anything from you. I never did. I never expected to see you again."

"Clearly." Every line of her body was defiant, but as Malak studied her, it wasn't her defiance that got to him. It was that other thing. That spark that had bloomed between them in that bar long ago. The same fire still licked through him, and he didn't like that at all. Wanting this woman would only complicate matters further. "But now I have returned. What I can't understand is why you care so little for your own child you would consign him to a life of hardship rather than involve me."

She let out a crack of laughter that felt a little too much like a slap. "Hardship? Did *you* just open your mouth and say something to me about hardship? What would you know about it?"

"You must know that I can provide for him in ways that you can only dream about. What mother wouldn't want that?"

"My son wants for nothing." Shona's voice was quiet again, but certain. Absolutely certain. "He's a happy kid. A good kid. And he's mine."

"What good is it to be yours if it means child care?" He nodded at the shoddy restaurant behind her. "A mother who must scramble for tips in a place like this?"

"Because an honest day's work is beneath you, obviously."

"Is this about honesty, Shona? Or your own bloody-mindedness?"

She rolled her eyes. Actually rolled her eyes, which Malak was not sure anyone had ever done *to* him in all his life.

"He's four years old because guess what? Sometimes when people have sex, babies come of it. I'm surprised a worldly man like you didn't know that."

"I used a condom." He had always used condoms. Always.

"They are not one-hundred-percent guaranteed. Apparently. And I dealt with the consequences of that all this time, all on my own. Except now you roll back into town talking about thrones and kings like I'm supposed to drop everything and what? Be grateful that you discovered we exist? I don't think so."

What bothered Malak the most about her words

wasn't her tone of voice, which bordered on scathing. It was the fact that nothing she said was untrue.

He hadn't looked back when he'd left. He'd remembered her and her charming innocence, but had it not been for his father and brother's abdications from the Khalian throne, something no one could possibly have predicted and Malak himself still did not quite believe, he would never have returned here.

But he didn't say that. He found he couldn't.

Because he didn't like what it said about him—and wasn't that funny? He had spent his whole life gleefully embracing the worst of his impulses. Was it his ascension to the throne that made it all seem squalid now?

Or was it the way Shona looked at him, as if *squalid* was all she saw?

"You could have reached out when you discovered you were pregnant," he said stiffly.

The way she looked at him then was not exactly friendly. But Malak preferred that to the quiet certainty with which she'd dismissed him as nothing but *a man in a bar*.

Maybe that was the real lesson here, he thought with entirely too much sharp self-awareness. He could stand anything save anonymity.

"How would I have done that?" Shona asked coolly. "You never told me your full name. You didn't leave me your telephone number. I discovered who you were entirely by accident."

"You mean tonight?"

"I mean I saw a picture of you in a magazine about six months later." She shook her head. "And no, before you ask, it did not cross my mind to try to chase down the Playboy Prince drowning in models across the world who came from some country I've never heard of. Why would I?"

Malak straightened from the side of the Range Rover. There were too many things competing inside of him for dominance, and he didn't know quite what to do with any of them.

He settled on fury. It felt cleanest.

"If you knew who I was, then you had no excuse."

"It was a one-night stand," Shona replied, still with that same damn cool. That—more than anything—told him how different she was from that smiling, bright girl he'd met on the bar stool next to his. And he refused to ask himself if he was to blame for that change, because he was fairly certain he wouldn't like the answer. "And as far as I could tell, you had those every night of the week. Why would you remember me?"

Why, indeed? And why was that a question Malak suddenly didn't want to answer?

"I remember you now," he told her with soft menace. "And even if I did not, the palace investigators found you all on their own. They informed me, in case I'd forgotten, that I was in New Orleans exactly nine months before you gave birth to a little boy who

looks a good deal like me. And I might be tempted
to believe in coincidences, especially because I've
never gone without protection in my life, but they do
not. It was simpler than I suspect you wish to know
to get a sample of the child's DNA to prove what is
already obvious at a glance."

Her brown gaze met his in a steady sort of challenge that no one else would dare. He told himself it
was one more problem with this woman—her obvious inability to recognize her place—but that was
not how it felt. "I thought you were supposed to be
the king. Don't you tell your people what to do?"

Malak didn't want this. He had never really
thought much of marriage at all, not for himself.
Not after a front-row seat to his parents' misera-
ble one. And he had certainly never planned to find
himself shackled to a woman he'd known for a single night long ago. He had not been raised to worry
about continuing the bloodline. But from the moment
Zufar had abdicated, Malak had found advisors in
his ear, throwing out the names of eligible women
of royal blood—Princess Amara of Bharathia, the
Lady Suzette, and so on until it was all a blur of
names and titles—and demanding he start thinking
about his heirs.

Until it appeared he already had one.

And that reminded him who he was. He was no
longer the Playboy Prince, the smirking star of a
thousand tabloid articles. He was the king, with com-

mitments to his people and their future whether he liked it or not, and it didn't matter what had happened in the past few years. The only thing that mattered was what happened now.

"I understand your reluctance," he told her, though he could tell that his tone was more cold than concerned by the way she stiffened. "But I am only here as a courtesy. I thought it would be better if I came to collect you myself instead of sending my men."

"You can't collect me. I'm not something you can pick up—"

She stopped, and the air changed between them. Something dark and dangerous seemed to loom there, just out of reach.

Malak did not state the obvious. That she was indeed something he could pick up, and he had.

But he might as well have yelled it.

"I should warn you that I have a limited amount of patience as it is," he said softly, though not particularly carefully. "While I am aware of my own culpability in this, the fact remains that there is no possibility that my son and heir will be raised apart from me. The kings of Khalia are raised in the palace, under the care of the traditional tutors, the better to prepare for their eventual role. That is how it has been for centuries. That is how it will remain."

She stood tall and still, her gaze on his and her hands in fists at her side. "My son is not a king."

"No, he is a prince." Malak gazed down at her,

every inch of him the royal he had always been, though he had largely ignored it. But here, now, it was as if his ancestors roared in his blood. "The crown prince of Khalia, in point of fact. All that remains is to give him legitimacy. What that means, I am afraid, is that you will have to marry me. Whether you like it or not."

Her breath left her in a kind of laugh. "I'm not going to marry you. I'm not going to hand my child over to you for random tutors to raise. You're delusional."

"That would make things easier for you, I'm sure. But I assure you, I am nothing of the kind."

"Does everyone in Khalia marry a complete stranger? Is that also how it's been for centuries?"

"As a matter of fact, many of the marriages in my family were arranged." Malak didn't think this was the time or place to comment on how those arrangements had worked out over time. His parents' stormy marriage being the premiere case in point. "We are royal, after all. My brother was raised as the crown prince and was betrothed to an appropriate princess since her birth."

Malak decided not to share how that had worked out, either. For either Zufar or Amira, the woman he'd been promised to but had not married, in the end. To say nothing of the half brother he'd never known he'd had, Adir, who had appeared from nowhere at their mother's funeral and had spirited

Amira away with him on the day of her wedding to Zufar.

None of those inconvenient truths would help him make his point here, to Shona. "Marrying strangers isn't the barrier for me you might imagine."

"Well, it's a barrier for me," she threw at him. "Because I'm not completely insane."

"You have a choice before you, Shona. You can fight me all you like, but you will lose. And either way, I will be returning to Khalia with my son." Malak let that sink in. He watched the way her chest rose and fell, too fast, and knew his edicts weren't exactly landing well. "You can stay behind, if you wish. But I cannot tolerate any trouble or scandal. The kingdom cannot survive any more turmoil. So you need to ask yourself—are you willing to give up your child? To sign away all your rights and never speak of this again?"

"I would rather die," she gritted out at him.

Malak felt that his smile was much too thin, but he aimed it at her, anyway. "Then again, let me offer my congratulations. For your only other choice is to return to Khalia with us and take your place as my queen."

"I would rather—"

"Careful," Malak warned her, his voice hardly more than a growl. "What I'm offering you is a great honor, whether you see it that way or not. Be very, very sure that you want to offend me. Be at peace with the inevitable consequences."

Shona did not look anything like *peaceful*. "I'm not marrying you, Malak."

"You will," Malak said pitilessly. "Or you will remain behind, legally separated from your child and muzzled by a thousand contracts that ensure your silence, forevermore. Those are your choices."

"You can't force me to do any of these things," Shona threw at him, as if amazed he thought otherwise. As if she expected the dirty streets of New Orleans to rise up on her behalf. "You can't *make* me do anything!"

But Malak only smiled, and this time, it was real.

Because his patience was finally at an end.

CHAPTER THREE

THEY LANDED IN Khalia the next morning.

Shona felt very much the way she had that morning long ago, when she'd woken up in the most sumptuous, luxurious hotel suite she'd ever seen in her life to find herself all alone. She'd felt...deliciously battered, and somehow made new.

And she'd had no idea how she, who had never had any intention of falling into bed with a stranger and ending up alone and pregnant—too many examples of girls who'd taken that path in foster care had soured her on those choices—had found herself there.

Which was to say, she could remember every gloriously carnal detail, but she didn't understand how she'd surrendered all of herself so heedlessly to a man she'd never laid eyes on before that night.

At least this time she could track the sequence of events.

Malak had announced that he was finished with their conversation. And more, that his next stop would be her friend's house—because, of course, he knew about Ursula—to pick up his son.

He kept saying that. *His son*. It made Shona's sight turn red at the edges. It made her feel something like violent, temper rushing through her like a river.

That it was only the simple truth made it worse.

"You can either be a part of our first meeting or not," he'd told her, all steel and disregard, and she'd wanted to scream at him. She'd wanted to beat on him with her fists. She'd wanted to make him deeply, desperately sorry he'd come back into her life.

But she'd wanted to protect Miles a whole lot more than she'd wanted any of that.

So she'd hated herself for it, but she'd gotten in the car.

There was no pretending it wasn't another surrender. And as much as Shona wanted to deny it—as much as she told herself that this was about Miles and nothing else—that wasn't what it had felt like, tucked away in the back of a much-too-comfortable Range Rover with Malak.

Malak, whom she'd wanted to tear apart with her fingers, but didn't dare—and not because of the armed men who watched her with cold, narrow eyes. But because she honestly didn't know, even as angry as she'd been then, what she would do if she allowed her fingers access to that hard, lean, athletic body. She couldn't trust that a swing of her fist might not turn into a betraying caress.

It was one more reason to hate herself.

And then they'd arrived at Ursula's little apartment on the outskirts of the Garden District, and she'd ordered herself to stop obsessing about Malak.

Because the other shoe had dropped. Squarely on her head, as she should have expected it would. And now she had to tell her little boy that his father was here.

The father she'd told him he didn't have.

"Let me bring Miles down to you," she'd said when the driver parked the SUV, something a little darker than mere panic beating at her.

And she'd felt more than seen the way Malak had looked at her from where he lounged there in the back seat beside her. His gaze *felt* dark and dangerous, like a hand at her throat.

"Do not make me chase you," he'd said quietly. Too quietly. "I doubt you would enjoy what would happen if it was you alone trying to escape me. But Shona, hear this, if nothing else. If you make me hunt my son—if you force me into the role of predator before I have ever even laid eyes on him and make that our first experience of each other—I will never forgive you."

"Maybe I don't want your forgiveness," she'd thrown back at him, because she couldn't quit. She couldn't hold her tongue. Maybe she was made wrong, the way many a foster parent had suggested over the years.

Made to be alone, they'd said. Made to make everyone around her happy to leave her be.

She'd taken pride in that all her life. She'd had no idea why it had felt so different then, as if she was a monster, somehow. When she hadn't been the one making all the threats.

"I have no doubt about that." Malak's voice had still been much too quiet, and Shona hadn't mistaken the malice in it. "But you must ask yourself if you wish your son to pay the inevitable price along with you."

And that was the trouble, of course. There was a part of her that had wanted nothing more than to snatch up Miles and make a run for it. No matter how it ended, just to prove that Malak couldn't show up like this and order her around, much less make these *pronouncements* just because he was a big deal where he came from.

But she had no idea how she would explain that to a four-year-old.

And so she'd climbed the stairs to Ursula's apartment, feeling very much as if she was marching to her own execution. She'd let herself in the way she always did and had wanted…some kind of poignant moment, maybe. Something to prove that she wasn't made to be alone—that she and Ursula were friends, after all. That her life was more than a sticky restaurant, pathetic tips and the kind of eternal solitude that made her bones ache sometimes.

But Ursula sat on her ratty old couch, a cigarette in her hand and her gaze on the television screen flickering on the wall across the room. She barely looked up. She gave a distracted wave when Shona offered her a slightly overdone goodbye, and that was it. Shona picked up a sleeping Miles and sighed a little as he settled his sweet face into the crook of her neck.

Ursula would miss the child care. But Shona knew better than to imagine the other woman would miss *her*.

Then she'd walked back downstairs. To her doom.

"He's asleep," she'd said in a hushed tone as she made it back down to the street to find Malak standing there beside his Range Rover again, as if he'd been readying himself to chase her through the streets of the Garden District, if necessary.

She'd expected an argument. A demand, perhaps, that Shona wake up Miles right there and then so that Malak could enact whatever tender, imaginary father/son reunion he was carrying around in his head.

But instead, he only gazed at her and the child she held so securely against her for what felt like an eternity, his expression fierce. Almost…arrested.

"He might wake up when we go back to my house and pack his things," she'd told him, not at all certain why she'd felt the need to solve this issue for him. To make it okay that this was happening when she'd never wanted it to happen in the first place.

But he was Miles's father. She had to remember that. She told herself that was the only reason she felt the need to give Malak what he wanted.

"We have no need to return to that house," Malak said. And Shona had been certain she wasn't imagining the way he emphasized *that house*, as if the very words were distasteful to him. "My men have already collected your personal effects."

"There's nothing wrong with my house," Shona had retorted, with a little more heat than necessary. She'd cradled the back of Miles's head with her hand, as if she'd needed to protect him from any aspersions Malak had wanted to cast on the home she'd worked so hard to give him. "I've always been proud and lucky to have it."

"We will endeavor, you and I, to provide you with far better opportunities for pride, I think." Malak's voice had been blistering, for all it was soft against the thick night, and his gaze had been so dark it had almost hurt. "And a far, far better environment in which to raise my son."

My son.

Shona had bitten her tongue. Because what else could she do? It was bewildering and more than a little awful in ways she didn't even know how to take on board, but there was no denying the fact that it was really, truly happening. Malak had really returned and, just as she'd always feared, taken control.

Of her. Of Miles. Of everything.

She'd believed that he'd sent his henchmen to pack up her whole life as if it was that easily erased, at his whim. Just as she'd believed that he would absolutely take Miles from her if she fought him.

The man she remembered from the night of her twenty-first birthday had been charming. But even then, she'd been aware that there was a core of steel beneath all that laziness and sensuality. She'd seen hints of it, here and there. She'd remembered it, somehow, though he'd been nothing but obliging and kind.

But now there was no charm, no kindness. There was nothing but steel and command, and she wondered how she'd ever imagined there was anything else. How she'd possibly fallen for the notion that he'd been easy, lazy or mild in any way.

He had not demanded that she hand over Miles in the car, as she'd feared. Nor did he take the sleeping child from her when they arrived at an airfield on the banks of Lake Pontchartrain and boarded the private jet that waited there, sporting the lavish insignia of the Royal House of Khalia.

She didn't know what was wrong with her that she saw these things as evidence that Malak was…not a good man, necessarily, but better than she'd imagined. Better, certainly, than she'd worried he might be after all these years of lying awake at night, stressing over this exact reality coming to pass.

You're pathetic, she'd told herself, but that hadn't helped a thing.

Much less changed it.

Once on board the private jet, that had reminded Shona a little too much of that absurdly luxurious hotel suite where she'd created this mess five years ago, Malak had showed her to one of its state rooms with a courtesy she'd found only slightly exaggerated, and had watched her, his dark green eyes glittering with an emotion she'd been afraid to name as she'd laid Miles on the bed. He'd moved closer then, and Shona had held her breath, but all he'd done was stand to the side of the bed and gaze down at the sleeping child.

His son, whom he'd never met.

And Shona had never missed him. She might have wished that things had been different across these last years, but she had never missed Malak, specifically. She had never imagined him and Miles, father and son together, or wasted her time dreaming of happy families. That was one more casualty of her foster-care experiences. She didn't believe in happy families. She never had. She wasn't even sure she believed in fathers, come to that, because that line on her birth certificate had been left blank and she'd never met any men deserving of that title during her eighteen years as a ward of the state.

So she had no words for what had washed over her then, like some kind of flash flood. It had been devastating and life-altering, and it had happened too fast. It had been almost too intense to bear. It had been something primal.

There was something about the way Malak had looked down at Miles. Or maybe it had been the simple fact of the three of them in one room—her little boy and both of his parents, for the first time.

Shona had never had the same experience. She hadn't known it was something she'd craved, hard and deep, as if her bones had been crying out for it all this time.

She felt something inside of her that she couldn't even name…turn over. And hum a little, as if something she hadn't known was lost and hadn't thought to miss had been returned to her, at last.

And when she'd looked up again, when she'd dared, Malak had turned that unreadable dark green gaze of his on her.

Shona had no idea why the only thing she'd wanted to do then was apologize. She hadn't even known for what.

She'd felt the air between them drawn tight. Thick with emotion, maybe. Or regrets. All that lost time, those lost years, stolen from the little boy who slept innocently between them.

Shona hadn't understood the power of family, of blood, until that moment. Until she found herself yearning for things she'd never wanted, ever.

"Malak…" She hadn't known what she'd meant

to say. Only that it had been clawing at her throat, demanding she open her mouth and give into it—

"We will take off momentarily," Malak had told her, his voice as cold as his eyes had been hot. And accusing. "And when we land, we will be in the capital city of Khalia. I suppose it is as good a place as any to meet my son."

And Shona had stayed there in that state room, feeling ripped apart in ways that didn't make sense. Because it wasn't that Malak was taking her away from the only life she'd ever known—though she imagined that would hit her, sooner or later. It wasn't that he had appeared in the first place, making his demands and his outlandish claims. That wasn't what had kept her awake, though her eyes had been gritty and glassy as she'd stared up at the smooth ceiling. It was that look on his face as he'd gazed down at Miles.

Shona had lived the whole of her life without ever loving another person.

That was how she'd grown up. That was what she'd learned one foster home at a time. She'd relied on herself, that was all, but she'd never believed that love was a real thing that could exist between real people. Until Miles.

He'd come into the world and cracked her wide open. His birth had changed everything. It was as if she'd lived all her life in a dark little house, curtains drawn tight over boarded-up windows, and Miles had punched through each and every one of them to let in the sun.

She knew the look that had been on Malak's face. She'd recognized it. It was that same disbelieving, bone-deep love for his own child that had no equal. It was like a heart attack that didn't kill, a cancer that settled there sweet and insistent in the bones. It was every breath. It was a kind of madness.

She'd seen it all over his face.

And Shona knew her way around bitterness. She welcomed it, come to that, because it made certain there were few unpleasant surprises out there in an uncaring world. But as bitter as she might have been, she wasn't sure she had it in her to truly hate a man who loved her child like that.

That deeply. That truly. And that instantaneously.

And she didn't know what that meant for her. Or how on earth she meant to survive whatever was coming next if she didn't have the strength and purity of hating Malak to guide her.

But then they landed, and Miles was awake again, and all her dithering had led to nothing. Save a sleepless night, which left her feeling hollowed out and scraped raw as she led her son off the plane.

Because it was that or bar herself in the state room and hope for…what, exactly?

There was no good answer to that. So she took Miles's hand in hers and answered his excited ques-

tions as best as she could, and walked off the plane
into the new life she'd never wanted in the first place.

Shona had never been anywhere. She'd been born
and abandoned in New Orleans and she'd assumed
she would die there, too. She'd always been practical, because anything else led directly to pain and
heartbreak, so she'd long ago stopped dreaming of
things that she could never have—something she'd
always thought was her best trait. She'd been proud
of the fact that no one could hurt her. No one could
even come close.

She'd been bulletproof.

And yet the moment they stepped outside the con-
fines of the jet, a thousand dreams she'd forbidden
herself to have seemed to flow back into her, like
yet another dangerous flood. All those nights she'd
spent curled up in a ball, blocking out the sounds of
the latest horrible house some stranger had insisted
she called her home. All those dreams she would
have denied she'd ever entertained in the morning,
of faraway places and exotic skies.

She'd never seen a sky like the one spread out
before her at the top of the jet's stairs, stretching on
and on like hope. It was vast and impossibly blue,
brighter and more intense than any she'd ever seen.
And it took her long moments to understand that
she wasn't simply breathless, but that there was no
moisture in the air. The landscape that stretched out
in all directions, rippled and sinuous and the color

of clay pots, was a desert—there were no swamps, no levees, no gnarled old cypress trees wreathed in Spanish moss, no murky bayou waters filled with alligators and secrets.

It was like being on another planet.

Shona wasn't sure if she wanted to laugh or cry, or what emotion it was inside of her that seemed to be clawing its way out against her will—but Miles had no such affliction.

He tugged at her hand and she let him go.

And she couldn't help feeling that it was filled with portent, that letting go. That it was an act of foreboding, of premonition—

"Be careful," she called out, but it was a lost cause.

Because Miles was already moving. Running. He barreled down the steps of the jet and onto the tarmac. And it was like watching a kind of nightmare, Shona thought. It was slow motion and felt as if it had all been preordained. That every step her little boy took had been planned, exactly like this.

Because Malak waited there at the bottom, alone.

Shona noticed that there were no guards arrayed around him even as she watched Miles run headlong into this future she couldn't prevent. And she knew, somehow, that Malak had emptied the tarmac. That his guards no doubt waited for him in the small airport hangar she could see to one side of the runway, but had cleared out, the better not to overwhelm a four-year-old.

And she had been alone too long, she thought as she made it down the stairs and stepped onto the tarmac herself. Or perhaps she couldn't work out how to breathe in the desert air, or think critically in the glare of all the Khalian sun that danced over her skin. But try as she might, she just wasn't sure she had it in her to hate this man who'd put her son's feelings first, without even having to be asked.

Just as she didn't have it in her to do anything but watch—more touched than she wanted to admit—as with no more than a single swift glance her way that shook her to the core, no matter its brevity, Malak crouched down to put himself on Miles's level, and at long last met his own son.

CHAPTER FOUR

TWO WEEKS LATER, Shona was ready to scream. Knock down the palace walls, if possible. Raze the royal city to the ground all around her.

And get the hell out of there before she imploded.

Or worse.

It wasn't that anything had gone horribly wrong. She wasn't treated badly, the way she'd half worried she would be—the way she had been more times than she could count when she'd been shifted to a new foster home. The truth of the matter was that the royal Palace of Khalia was by far the nicest place Shona had ever seen.

Or imagined, for that matter.

She thought about the traditional exteriors of palaces that a person expected from movies and advertising, and realized she'd never thought about what they might look like inside. And if she had, she never would have imagined all the *gold*.

She had been treated like a queen from the start, whether she wanted to become one or not. She and

Miles had been bundled into their own car after those moments on the tarmac that Shona still couldn't think about without her heart seeming to catch in her chest, and then swept off into the capital city that rose from the dunes as if it had been fashioned from the same sand.

"Is that really my dad?" Miles had asked in wonder, as if a father was a surprise adventure Shona had arranged for him—like a carnival ride.

"It really is," Shona had replied in as even a tone as she could manage.

And she'd braced herself for questions. Recriminations. Or explanations she wasn't prepared to give. But that wasn't Miles. He accepted the addition of a father and a trip abroad to a magical new place the way he accepted any gift—as if it had all always been meant to be his.

Shona hadn't known whether she should have been as grateful for that as she was. She was sure it said terrible things about her as a mother that she'd raised a child who could so easily…shift. From no father at all to an actual father who happened to be the king of a foreign land made of sand in the blink of an eye.

While Miles had chattered on in delight, the way he might about an action figure, Shona had stared out the window without knowing where to look. She'd braced herself to answer all the questions that Miles might fire at her, but he was busy telling her

that *his* father was a *king*. So she stared at the build-
ings they passed as they entered the city through the
high, imposing walls, but none of the structures she
saw seemed to make any sense. All the shapes were
wrong. Or different, anyway, from what she knew.

And she still hadn't managed to take a deep
breath.

The palace itself was worse. Or a wonder, anyway, and Shona hardly knew how to take it in. Her
urge was to turn around and leave—to get the hell
away before she could like it too much or want to
stay, because she knew better than that—but escape
wasn't on offer.

She was a foster kid, she kept telling herself, holding tight to Miles's hand as they walked inside the
gleaming white palace that was the most beautiful
thing she'd ever seen, graceful and immense at once.
She'd been abandoned when she was six days old,
literally left outside a bar like a bag of trash. She had
no business in a royal palace.

She kept expecting someone to notice.

Everywhere she looked there was marble and
gold, and then more marble and gold. Though there
had been desert in all directions outside, the palace was filled with green things, bright flowers and
water everywhere. It was bright and yet cool, despite
the heat just beyond its walls. Glorious fountains
flowed into pools and cascaded into gardens, heedless of the rolling dunes outside. The floors looked

clean enough to eat off, unlike the battered streets of the French Quarter back home.

And worse, every person she passed bowed their head to her. Even wearing that same old uniform from her job back in the restaurant on the other side of the planet, they bowed.

She couldn't help thinking that once they realized what a mistake Malak was making, they'd hate her for that most of all. They'd call her an imposter—and they'd be right.

But no one seemed to share her concerns.

"This is completely unnecessary," she'd said to the woman who'd waited for her upon their arrival and introduced herself as Shona's very own servant. And it was possible she'd sounded a little…shrill. "I don't need servants of any kind and you certainly don't need to bow like that when you talk to me."

"You are queen—"

"I most certainly am not. I'm not queen. I'm not going to be queen."

If the servant, whose name was Yadira, was taken back by Shona's vehemence, she'd given no sign. She looked as if she could be Shona's age, or a little older, and there was something about the robes she wore that made her every movement seem extrafeminine—or maybe it was just that Shona had slept in her black T-shirt and red skirt and was now shuffling around *a palace* dressed like a French Quarter waitress. It was getting to her.

Or, possibly, it was everything else that had happened since Malak had walked back into her life.

"You are the mother of the crown prince of Khalia," Yadira had said quietly, her dark eyes touching Shona's, then lowering. "How else should you be treated?"

Shona had been too overtired then—or that was what she told herself—to argue. And she certainly couldn't explain the chaos inside of her.

She'd expected them to take Miles from her like every dramatic movie she'd ever watched. She'd steeled herself for a screaming battle, but it hadn't happened. Yadira had delivered them to a suite of rooms that rambled over what seemed to be an entire wing of the palace, and was bigger than all the places Shona had ever lived…put together. Yadira had showed them around, pointing out a series of living areas, a private pool, balconies everywhere, dens and bedrooms and her own stocked kitchen should she feel compelled to make herself a snack… or, say, a twelve-course meal. She showed Shona what she called "your bedchamber," which was actually another set of rooms inside the suite—a private sitting room, a bathroom that was larger than her house back in New Orleans and that sported a tub that could fit several people and enjoyed a view over a rambling, walled garden, as well as a door she didn't even open that Yadira told her led to her dressing rooms. Plural.

But the only room Shona cared about was the one that led directly from her bedroom into what Yadira called the nursery. It was a bedroom for Miles as well as his own bathroom and playroom, and in yet another sitting room, a set of nannies who all exclaimed over him as if he was the center of the universe.

That Shona might have agreed only made it worse.

"He doesn't need any nannies," Shona had told Yadira fiercely, ignoring the fact that Miles, always a joyful boy and completely at ease wherever he went, seemed perfectly happy with all the attention.

"Of course not, mistress," Yadira had replied mildly. Even deferentially. "They are only here to aid you. And only so much as you wish."

"I don't wish."

Yadira had nodded as if this was perfectly acceptable and, even more, as if it made sense.

"Are you certain you do not wish to refresh yourself after your long journey?" She'd waved a hand toward the nannies, who were sitting on the floor with Miles and making him laugh. "We are all strangers to you, I understand. But you do not need to trust us. What you can trust is that the king would not permit a single hair on his son's head to be harmed in any way. And that his reaction to such an outrage would be swift and terrible."

And that, Shona had believed. Or maybe she'd just been too damn tired. Or any of the other maddening and overwhelming things that swirled around inside of her and nearly made her doubt her own name, standing in the middle of the kind of luxury that made her very uneasy indeed.

As if she would…break it. All of it. Or worse, it would somehow break her. Ruin her. Make her soft and dreamy and easily knocked down.

And what would happen to her—and her child—if she couldn't get back up?

"Miles," she'd called. "Do you want to come with me while I clean up?"

But Miles had new toys and a father who was a king and more, a group of new friends who found him *delightful*.

"No," he told her, without even looking her way. "I'm playing."

And that was how Shona had found herself alone in that endless, rambling bathroom, also done up in marble and golds and shot through with deep blue tiles. And maybe she was already getting soft—or maybe it was just the long flight—but she didn't have it in her to deny herself that tub, with the jets and the steps and the window over the beautiful jewel of a garden with the desert looming out there in the distance. And when she was done, she helped herself to the array of cosmetics and products that lined the acres of sink. She spent some time on her hair. She tried to hide the sleeplessness and the worry, until she asked herself who, exactly, she was trying to hide that from.

And when she walked back out into what she couldn't quite believe was supposed to be her bedroom when it could house half a city, she found her waitress uniform was gone. And in its place, spread out over the vast sea of a bed, were the kinds of clothes that made her feel something a lot more worrisome than simply hollow.

None of this is real, she told herself, her heart slamming into her ribs as she looked at the sorts of dresses girls like her didn't bother dreaming about, because they were so out of reach.

Or even if it was real, she understood it had to be temporary. Or the kind of test some foster parents liked to set up. Like the one family she'd been with who had made strict rules about mealtimes and then had put out fresh, fragrant doughnuts in the kitchen to see who would fall into the trap.

Shona had never been fooled by such things.

If something looked too good to be true, it was probably put there specifically to hurt her. She'd learned that a long time ago.

Dressed in nothing but a towel and her own uneasiness, Shona walked over to the dressing-room door, which led into what she supposed was meant to be a closet—though it bore no resemblance to any closet she'd ever seen. It was a large room with seating in the middle, as if previous occupants had grown tired in the midst of dressing themselves in endless finery and had required breaks. And instead of wearing the absurdly fancy dress that had been laid out for her as if she was some kind of fairy princess, she dug around until she found something more reasonable. None of her own clothes were anywhere to be found, but she came up with a pair of trousers that fit her perfectly and felt good when she pulled them on, and a kind of tunic in a shade of blue she was forced to admit made her skin seemed to shine from within. Everything fit her and, worryingly, she felt comfortable in these clothes that didn't belong to her.

She was certain she hadn't mistaken the way Yadira had sighed when she'd caught sight of her after she'd eventually found her way back into Miles's playroom—where he hadn't seemed to notice she was gone.

But she hadn't changed. And that was how she'd been dressed when she was taken into the private dining room of the king of Khalia for the first time.

Who looked even less like the man she had met on a bar stool five years previously. He'd changed out of that suit he'd been wearing into something that she couldn't possibly have named, white and flowing, but which seemed to suit him. It made him seem…more. More dangerous. More demanding. More impossibly beautiful without having to waste a single smile.

He was so clearly and obviously a king that it made her stomach somersault around inside her.

"What on earth are you wearing?" Malak had

asked her, in an idle sort of way she didn't believe at all.

He'd been lounging there on a pile of brightly colored pillows in front of a low table laden with trays of food, but she couldn't really take all that in. Much less the balcony behind him that offered sweeping views all over the city that looked so alien to someone born and bred in the bayou. Instead, she found herself focusing on the laughter she was sure she could see in that dark green gaze of his, glittering at her.

It made her feel things she didn't want to acknowledge. She'd told herself she didn't feel anything but anger. "I want my own clothes."

"You can't have them," Malak had replied in that same idle way. As if it wasn't even a question. "I am sure they served you well in whatever existence it was you carved out in that dreadful place, but you are in Khalia now. None of those clothes are appropriate for the role you must assume here."

She'd straightened her spine as if she planned to fight him with her hands. As more than a little of her wanted to do, right here and now. Her fingers twitched. "I haven't agreed to marry you, Malak. I haven't even agreed to eat with you. I don't know why you think you can just ignore the things you don't want to hear."

His mouth curved a little at that, but he didn't argue.

Which, in retrospect, Shona found even more alarming.

"You are the mother of the crown prince of Khalia," he'd said, and she didn't really care for the exaggerated patience in his voice. Much less the echo of what Yadira had said to her—telling her exactly what the party line was here in this fanciful place and more, where it had come from. "Regardless of how you feel about that role, it, too, comes with certain expectations."

Shona had sniffed. "Your expectations sound like your problem, not mine."

"And yet I think you will find that my expectations are very often treated as law," he'd said in that same mild way that it had occurred to her belatedly was misdirection. Because nothing about him was mild, especially as he lounged there before her, looking lazy again when she knew it was a lie. And if she paid closer attention, she could hear the steel beneath it. "Whether you like it or not, Khalia is an absolute monarchy."

But Shona had never been one to back down in the face of defeat, certain or otherwise. "I'm not entirely certain that your laws pertain to me. Is there an American embassy? I'd like to talk to them about any number of things. Such as how you got me into the country in the first place, since neither Miles nor I have passports."

He'd smiled as if she delighted him, and Shona

hated the part of her that pulsed at that, as if that was what she'd wanted all along. "You are mistaken. Both you and Miles have passports. I ordered their issue myself."

"How could you order—?"

But she cut herself off. Because it had taken her a moment, but she understood. He wasn't talking about American passports.

"Congratulations," Malak murmured, those dark green eyes of his gleaming. "You and my son are Khalian citizens."

She'd breathed in, then out, and she'd still felt unsteady. "Your congratulations are a lot like getting sucker punched. In case you wondered."

"How strange. Most women liken the faintest shred of my attention to a gift from the heavens. Perhaps there is something the matter with you."

"I can think of a great many things that are the matter with me," Shona had said tightly. "Every one of them another reason I can't possibly stay here."

But Malak had only shrugged, as if the subject was closed and he'd grown bored with the discussion.

The security detail hadn't given her the message she got then. The private jet, the palace—all of that had registered, certainly, but it hadn't truly penetrated. Even the clothes he wore that so clearly marked him as who he'd claimed to be. Because this was the moment it really hit Shona that this man— the one-night stand she'd been sure she would forget eventually, despite her son's dark green eyes—was really and truly a king. And not a king in the tabloid sense, all silly highbrow scandals and the dedication of war memorials. But an old-school king of dungeons and orders from on high. The kind of king who could demand anything and whole populations would leap to do his bidding.

A real king, in other words.

The truth of it shuddered through her, bringing heat and what she assured herself was dismay.

"You're welcome to leave at any time," King Malak told her in that same tone that reminded her he was well and truly finished discussing the matter, in case she'd had any doubt. "I will instruct the guards to escort you to the royal airfield and fly you back the moment you wish to go, with my compliments. But Miles stays."

So Shona had stayed, too, of course. It wasn't as if there was any other option.

And because she stayed, she was forced into a role she had never wanted. Not that anyone had asked her what her feelings on the subject might have been.

Every morning, Yadira woke her and they engaged in the same routine. Yadira would lay out clothes befitting the queen that Shona was not and Shona would ignore them, marching over to her dressing room and rifling through it until she found something—anything—that approximated the jeans and T-shirt she would have worn if she could. That

meant a great many tunics and trousers, but it was
better than the alternative. Yadira would then pretend
she did not disapprove of this while serving Shona
and Miles their breakfast near one of the fountains
in their expansive suite.

If she squinted, it wasn't terribly different from
the mornings she'd shared with Miles back home.
The two of them had often eaten breakfast together,
then set about their days. But instead of rushing
through a breakfast that was often no more than cold
coffee she didn't have time to microwave, then rac-
ing off to the cleaning job that she'd taken during
the hours that Miles was in preschool to help make
ends meet, she was able to enjoy a meal and strong
coffee. Miles did as he pleased as well, spending his
days playing with his nannies, and learning from
them, too, as Shona had been informed when she'd
claimed he needed more structure.

"He is getting personal attention from his nannies,
all of whom are highly trained in child development,"
Malak had informed her in that high, holy-king voice
of his when she'd complained to him at one of those
meals she refused to eat. "It is the same education I
received at his age and yes, there is a great deal of
playing as well. Do you have actual concerns about
his development, Shona? Or is it that you dislike losing control?"

She had dared not answer that the way she longed
to do.

And besides, she had her own horrors to fill her days. Shona was forced into what Yadira called comportment classes.

"I don't need classes," she'd told Malak, coldly and with fury.

"Whether you do or not, you must take them if you wish to stay here," he'd replied. She still refused to eat with him. She stood there in the center of his dining room, pillows everywhere, candles flickering, and the balcony doors open to let the night in. She declined all offers—and demands—to sit. And she thought her stubbornness was getting to him. She could see it in that glittering heat in his gaze. She interpreted it as a victory. "Or you can fly back to New Orleans tomorrow. Your call."

"Do you ever get tired of making threats?"

He'd smiled. "I am the king, Shona. I do not make threats. My wishes are commands and my preferences law."

Which meant Shona suffered through the stupid classes, such as they were. A week into it, she couldn't tell which of them hated the experience more—her or her advisors, who openly despaired of her.

"You must at least try," they would tell her.

"I don't want to try," she would reply.

And then she would smile the way she'd learned to smile at the tourists in the French Quarter to get better tips, until she could see the tempers they were all too well-trained to lose in her presence.

The things she refused to try grew all the time. She refused to learn which fork to use at a table. She refused to learn how to wear the scarves and robes they laid out before her, because she refused to blend in with the people here. She refused to pay any attention to the tiny details that comprised the sort of diplomacy queens were expected to wield, because she refused to become that queen. She was uninterested in learning how to walk appropriately. How to stand fetchingly. How to address heads of state, or not, depending on local customs.

She might have had to take the classes. Or sit through them, anyway. But that didn't mean she needed to distinguish herself as any kind of honor student. She'd taken a similar approach in all the high schools she'd found herself in as she'd bounced around from one home to the next in her last few years in the system.

Because one thing she knew well was that it was much, much worse to try hard for things that other people could take away on a whim. It was better not to try, not to want, not to break her own heart.

"You will embarrass the king," her teachers warned her, in tones of ever-deepening concern.

"I'm all right with that," she would reply serenely.

Miles, on the other hand, was thriving.

He loved the palace. He loved that he finally had a father. He loved his father heedlessly and wholeheartedly, in fact, and much as Shona might have hated her circumstances, she couldn't hate that. Miles loved his many nannies and teachers, all of whom doted on him as if he was truly the most delightful child alive—which he was, of course. In Shona's own, personal opinion. He loved all the new and exciting things he got to see and talk about every day. He loved that he had a grandfather, too, the sad old man who moved about the palace like a ghost in the wake of his wife's death and who barely replied to polite greetings.

Miles was fine. Happy, even.

It was Shona who couldn't fit in. Shona who was…wrong.

Like every foster home she'd ever found herself in, she reminded herself darkly. She'd survived them all. She would survive this, too.

"When will this defiance end?" Malak asked her one night.

He'd made their dinners even more painful. He'd decreed that they would all eat together as a family. Again, it was that word that had never meant anything to her and yet resonated inside of her in ways she couldn't entirely understand. She worried that it was a word that meant so much she couldn't look at it directly—and so Shona was forced to bite the bullet and pretend everything was fine as long as Miles was there. And it almost was. Miles would chatter away happily while Shona glared at Malak across gold plates and heaping platters of food.

And the moment Miles's beloved nannies came to spirit him away, Shona would stand up and resume her stubborn refusal to take part in anything that didn't directly benefit her child.

"When will you stop pretending I'll ever be your queen?" Shona asked in return that night. "That's when you can expect my defiance to stop. Not before."

"I'm only interested in learning if there's a time-table." Malak sat back on his usual pile of pillows, looking entirely too at ease. "Because, Shona, I don't mind telling you, this is all quite boring."

"Heaven forbid. I wouldn't want to bore you." She rolled her eyes. "What could be worse than that?"

"I can think of a great many things that are worse than that," he said, much too softly.

She wasn't a fool. She could hear the warning in his voice.

But she ignored it.

"I can't," she said. Unwisely.

Because Malak smiled at her.

And then rose to his feet in a single, simple move-ment that did nothing but highlight his masculine grace in ways she could feel inside of her.

She could *feel* it. *Inside* her.

Her heart leaped toward her throat. Her stomach dropped toward her feet.

Run, something inside urged her—but her feet seemed nailed to the floor.

"What are you doing?" she asked, though she

hardly sounded like herself. She was only grateful she'd managed not to stammer.

But that seemed like a small and insubstantial victory indeed when that smile of his deepened. And turned something like fierce.

"It occurs to me that I've been going about this all wrong," Malak said with a quiet ferocity she could feel in her bones.

And everywhere else.

"I don't know what that means, but—"

"What is that saying?" he asked, but she knew he wasn't really asking. The look in his eyes was hot. And hard. And it made her want to do nothing at all but melt. "You get more flies with honey than with vinegar, is that not so?"

But he didn't wait for her to come up with an answer.

He simply started toward her.

CHAPTER FIVE

MALAK WAS AT the end of his patience.

Until now, he hadn't actually known whether or not he was the sort of man who had patience in the first place. Much less if he could handle his patience being tested. Repeatedly. There had simply never been the opportunity to experiment, because for all that he'd been the largely ignored second son of the Khalian king, he had still always been a prince in his own right. Who would dare try his patience?

Since he'd arrived back in Khalia with Shona in tow, however, Malak had found numerous opportunities to experiment with his own ability to practice patience, for the first time in his life. And had subsequently discovered that there was not one part of self-restraint that he enjoyed.

Tonight was yet another night in this kingdom his forefathers had built out of the desert, now his to rule. He should have been deeply concerned about his people. Or his upcoming coronation, the formal ceremony to cement the transfer of power that had already occurred. He should have been worrying about the future in this land of his that could not rely on its oil exports forever.

And yet all he had on his mind, it seemed, was Shona.

Shona five years ago, when she'd walked into that hotel bar and stolen his breath. Shona in that gold dress that he could remember with shocking clarity—and especially when he'd taken it off her, inch by delectable inch. Shona beneath him in that wide bed in that hotel suite in New Orleans, her legs wrapped around his back.

Shona in a thousand carnal images from long ago.

But the real Shona was here, in front of him, every night.

And Malak found he didn't have it in him to wait any longer to get his hands on her. It had already been long enough.

It had been forever.

"What are you doing?" she asked again, with far more alarm in her tone.

He had stood, finally. Because he'd had enough of this foolhardy protest of hers—this absurd stubborn streak she seemed capable of indulging forever. He'd had no intention of letting it go on as long as it had, but part of him had wondered if she would really continue to push it. Part of him had wanted to see how long she could possibly maintain her commitment to something so obviously destined to fail.

Perhaps he shouldn't have doubted her. Because there was something about that belligerent chin of hers, forever tipped up as if to dare him to do something about it there and then. There was something about the way she looked at him, her brown eyes lit with challenge when most women—most people— in his life averted their gaze from his automatically, in deference to his exalted position.

He rather thought that if he let her, Shona would stand there forever, glaring at him for eternity.

At the end of the day, Malak was the one who couldn't take it.

He advanced on her now, aware that every part of him seemed to shift into a new kind of alertness when she backed away.

She had already taught him so much. That he was not a patient man, in any respect. That he disliked waiting for anything and was not a particular fan of rebellions, either. And he realized as he stalked toward her that it turned out he liked the chase, too.

Something he had never had occasion to discover before now.

Malak had never been given the opportunity to chase a woman. They were too busy flinging themselves at him and begging for the scraps of his attention.

But not Shona.

Never Shona.

She backed away, all the way across the room, and kept right on going onto the balcony that curved around this part of his private rooms, out into the soft desert night. He followed her, his movements unhurried. Easy.

Almost lazy, when he felt anything but.

Inside him, his heart was a drum. And there was something stirring in his blood, running through his veins, making him feel…lit up. Exhilarated, almost. In his chest and his greedy body alike.

"I have let this go on long enough," he told her, making no attempt to hide the satisfaction in his voice as she backed herself up against the stone balustrade and finally came to a stop. "And I must tell you, I admire your commitment. I do."

"I appreciate your admiration," Shona replied, and he took a little too much pleasure in that breathlessness he could hear in her voice. The wild sort of panic he could see on her face. "But I would appreciate it more from a distance."

"I have given you your distance." She had nowhere to go, and so he slowed his pace. But he didn't stop. He moved closer and closer, until he was caging her there, with nothing behind her but the great, gleaming canopy of his city. His kingdom. "I have allowed you your disrespect. No one else would dare behave the way you have, but I have permitted it. You may thank me for my magnanimity, if you wish."

He was fascinated by the way her chest rose and fell. Even in the tunic she wore like swaddling clothes, he could see how his proximity affected her. But he tested the theory, leaning ever closer, so she had to lean back and grip the stone beneath her to keep from toppling off into nothing.

Not that he would let her fall. But she didn't need to know that. A little fear and uncertainty would do her good.

"You're going to make me topple to my death," she gritted at him, which was in no way a sweet thank-you for the consideration he'd shown her. "Is that what you want?"

"Why would I want your death?" he asked, his voice lower than before. It was suggestive, being this close to her. When he could have leaned only the slightest bit forward to taste her, had he wished. "Unless it is a little death you mean. In the French sense of the term."

He could feel the heat that moved over her then, so bright and intense it singed them both. As if they were both imagining the way she'd come apart beneath his hands in that hotel bed, when Malak had taught her how very much her body thirsted for a man's touch.

For his touch.

"I would prefer not to die," she said, and her voice

was tighter than before. As if she was fighting not just Malak, but herself. "In a big or little way, thank you very much."

"Explain to me what you hope to gain with these displays." Malak stayed where he was, so close to her that his mouth was very nearly touching the satiny expanse of her neck. "Will you stand at attention forever when we are alone in a room? Will you refuse to wear clothes appropriate to your station, preferring to shuffle around the palace in these strange costumes that make the servants imagine you are mad? Where does it end?"

Her breath came raggedly, but when she spoke, her voice was cool. On some level, Malak admired it.

"It ends when I get to go home. Back to my actual life and away from all this...nonsense."

"You must know that will never happen," he said, and he didn't attempt to sugarcoat it. He stated it baldly. Without apology. And moved his head back as he did, so he could look her in the face.

She breathed in hard then, as if he'd hit her.

"I would very much like to blame you for concealing my son from me for all these years," Malak continued in the same stark way, there in the sweet dark with only a scant centimeter between their bodies. "But I find I cannot. I cannot pretend that I would have returned to find you under any other circumstances than these." He inclined his head. "I forgive it."

If he expected her to collapse into gratitude, he was in for a surprise. Because this was Shona. And she only glared at him in a kind of fury.

"How kind." Her voice dripped with sarcasm. Another thing he had never heard directed at him, not before this moment. Not until tonight. He hardly knew how to take it. "How lucky I am, indeed, to have been strong-armed into abandoning my entire life and everything I've ever known by a man so… *understanding*."

Malak laughed. "You do not seem to comprehend the situation you find yourself in, Shona. If I were less understanding, less kind, I would see that you were punished forever for this sin."

"I assumed this was the punishment." She sniffed. "A prison is a prison no matter how many clothes your minions fling across my bed every morning, Malak. You're holding me hostage no matter how you dress it up. No matter how you dress *me* up."

Malak was finished holding himself back. He'd had more than enough of holding himself in check and pretending her defiance did not prick at him, when all he wanted to do was get his hands on her. And reacquaint himself with that impossibly lush mouth and the lithe, curvy body that haunted him.

He needed to teach her how foolish she was to test him in such a blatant manner, as any woman from Khalia would have known full well. Malak had never understood Western women and their inability to understand these intimate battles. Or how best to fight them. Why confront a man head-on and lose when there were so many softer, more devastating ways to fight?

But the truth was, he wanted more than just another hot night with this woman who was now inextricably linked to him for as long as they both drew breath. He wanted more than sex.

Malak wanted nothing short of her total surrender.

"Tell me why I shouldn't touch you," he murmured, there on the balcony with his body so close to hers at last. She shivered, and he smiled. "Tell me why I should keep my hands to myself, Shona. When neither one of us wants it."

"I don't—"

"Tell me one thing that is not a lie, and who knows? I might let you go. Tonight."

Her dark eyes found his and held, and he was the one who had to repress a rolling sensation that was entirely too close to a shiver of his own. "I think you're the one who's lying."

Malak smiled at that and then he bent his head, pressing his mouth against the elegant ridge of her collarbone, there where the collar of her tunic exposed it. She jolted, but she didn't shove at him. She didn't push him away.

And she tasted better than he had remembered. Better than he'd dreamed. Rich, dark cream, sugar and need.

Heaven, he thought.

"Tell me," he urged her, with his lips against her skin at last. "Tell me what you need, Shona. And you might just get it."

"I want…" Her hands gripped the stone she leaned against, but as she spoke, her head tipped back to give him better access. "I want…"

"I know what you want," he told her, low and gravelly and no longer entirely in control.

And then he stopped playing and set his mouth to hers.

Everything went electric. Wild lightning and mad thunder.

She tasted like the kind of magic Malak had never believed in. White-hot. Lush and sweet. Her taste rolled through him, making him ache as if he'd never kissed a woman before. As if he never would again.

As if hers was the only taste he had ever known or could ever want.

He remembered this. The kick of her. The impossible sweetness. He remembered it, but now that she was right here again he couldn't understand how he had ever walked away from her in the first place.

Because Shona was addictive. She was perfect.

Malak angled his head, taking the kiss deeper, wilder, and making it far more intense. He fit his hands to the fine line of her jaw, and held her where he wanted her. He was suddenly, fiercely glad that she'd refused to wear the clothes he'd gotten for her because it meant he could feel her against him without the bother of all that extra fabric. He was hard and she was soft, and he fit himself against her as if they'd been made to be pieces of the same puzzle—

And that thought should have stopped him. It should have horrified him because he was a king, this was not a child's game and he did not believe in the kind of connection he felt with this woman. He had been raised by a man so heedlessly, hopelessly, sickeningly in love with his wife he'd failed entirely to notice either her indiscretions or his own children. Love had turned to grief and had ended his father's reign after his mother's death. Love had taken his brother, Zufar, from the throne shortly thereafter. Love was chaos and ruin, as far as Malak could tell. He had never wanted any part of that kind of sickness. Not even the faintest hint.

He had vowed that he would not allow love or any other foolish emotion to threaten his throne. Not him. He was the ignored son. The forgotten spare. He'd been the only one in his family who'd been capable of seeing just how terrible it had all become—even before his mother's death and the abdications that had followed.

Malak had vowed that he, the least likely king alive, would be the ruler his people deserved.

He should stop this. Now.

But he was too busy drowning in Shona's taste. The slick friction of her tongue against his.

She was like a drug.

And he wanted more and more, no matter what it cost him—

Shona pulled her mouth away from his then, bracing her hands against his chest as she gasped for breath.

And Malak forgot that he had taken the throne. That he was the king—or even that there was a kingdom to rule, out there somewhere in the dark.

Because all he cared about was Shona. And the dark, sweet joy of her taste.

He wanted more. He wanted everything.

"Malak…" she began, and her voice was different now. Hushed. Something like reverent, which should have been enough.

It almost was.

Because he knew that she was as shaken as he was that this thing between them was still so bold. So intense.

That it hadn't been the alcohol after all, all those years ago. The way he'd told himself when he'd left that morning, leaving her warm and naked in his bed and forcing himself not to look back. Not to linger. Not to test their connection one more time…

Malak didn't want to think about that. He just wanted more of her. That impossible taste of hers that licked through him like fire and made him feel like a stranger to himself.

He didn't wait to hear what she might say. What new, ridiculous barriers she might throw between them in her endless attempts to hold back the inevitable.

Malak sank down to his knees and heard the way her breath left her in a rush. He slid his hands up the length of her gorgeous legs, marveling in the feel of her. The play of lean muscle and soft curves. He hooked his fingers in the waistband of her foolish trousers. And he could feel, as well as hear, the harsh, intense way she was breathing, as if she was running somewhere—though she didn't move.

He paused, waiting for her to object, possibly. Or at the very least, question him.

But she didn't say a word. She didn't move. She only gazed down at him, her dark eyes gleaming.

Malak watched her lovely face as he peeled down her trousers, exposing her perfect legs to his view. He pulled them off, freeing one foot, then the other.

And he couldn't tell if it was her harsh breathing that filled his ears, or his own. But he didn't care. He set his hands to her legs again, tracing them and learning them as he smoothed his way back up the satiny soft skin he'd bared.

And when he made it to the delectable swell of her hips, he hooked his fingers around to the sweet, lush curve of her bottom, and pulled her toward him.

"Malak..." she said again.

And he interpreted that as an invitation. One he was more than happy to accept.

Malak smiled, then leaned close. He pushed the bit of lace she wore to the side and then he licked his way into the melting sweetness between her legs.

At last.

And he didn't know which one of them exploded. Or if it was both of them, in a rolling, endless burst of fire that threatened to consume them both.

He welcomed it.

He exulted in it.

And he wanted more.

Malak held her still, even as she bucked against him. He licked and he sucked. He used a hint of his teeth. And still, he couldn't seem to get enough of her. Her taste. That sweet, molten heat of hers that made him ache. Everywhere.

And the next time she called out his name, it sounded like a prayer. He felt her stiffen, then shatter into a hundred glorious pieces right there against his mouth.

But it still wasn't enough.

He shifted, sucking the center of her need into his mouth as he used one finger, then another, to test her wet, clinging heat.

Her hips rocked against him. The noises she made were delicious. Sweet and broken, as he took her from one shattering straight back into that fire.

And then he made her burn.

Again and again, until she was limp and sobbing.

Only then did he stop. Only then did he pull back, and smooth her lace panties back into place, and somehow keep himself from assuaging his own powerful need right then and there.

Because it was possible he was better at restraint than he imagined.

Malak stood, keeping his hand hooked around her arm so she wouldn't simply collapse over the side of the balcony. He felt more than a little deep, male satisfaction at how boneless she looked. How thrown. He handed her back her discarded trousers, and continued to prop her up as she blinked, looking delightfully dazed before she pulled them back on.

It took her a moment, because it was as if her limbs had ceased operating at her command.

"You can stand as long as you like," he told her, his voice as dark as all the wild and desperate greedy things that fought for supremacy inside him. But she had already taught him about patience. And need. Control. And the chase.

Now it was time to practice a different kind of restraint. Vinegar didn't work on Shona. She was too tough, deep into her bones, in ways Malak didn't particularly want to recognize. Too determined to meet anything that came at her with strength and defiance.

She was much too sure of herself in ways he

should have found appalling in a woman, especially one who would become his queen, but instead found he reluctantly admired in this one.

But it looked like honey was something she couldn't resist.

"Stand?" she asked, her voice thick. As shaky as the rest of her.

Malak didn't work too hard to hide his smile. "You can stand at every meal we have together until the end of time, if you so desire." He waited until her dark eyes, still a bit glassy and more than a little dazed, met his. "I will assume it is an invitation to partake of my favorite dessert. Do you understand?"

She looked mutinous. Or perhaps just a shadow of mutiny, lost there behind need and longing and the melting he could see written all over her.

And she was still breathing too hard when she answered him. "I don't like dessert."

Malak laughed, despite the heaviness in that part of him that urged him to simply lift her against him, carry her to his bed and be done with these games.

But he didn't, because he thought he understood this woman now. Or this game, anyway. And the fact that the only thing she was likely to understand was the way he could turn her own body against her. Because any direct approach would result in her direct resistance. But a kiss? That made her melt.

"No?" he asked mildly. "The way you came all over my face, calling my name, would suggest otherwise. But who am I to take away your illusions? Stand all you like, Shona. I not only welcome it. I have to say, I prefer it. I prefer this."

And he let go of her. Then left her there, shaking on his balcony, while he handled his own body in his shower.

Again.

CHAPTER SIX

SHONA STAGGERED OUT of Malak's private suite, not at all clear about how she was expected to walk when nothing about her body seemed to work the way it was supposed to any longer. The way it had when she'd walked in.

She felt taken over. Ruined in every respect, as if the longing that still moved through her was a kind of poison, corroding her from the inside out.

She nodded stiffly at the guards who stood at Malak's doors, and assured herself they couldn't possibly see what she had been up to inside. With him. They couldn't possibly see abandon written all over her.

Surrender, she told herself fiercely, did not have a scent.

Still, she was certain she could feel their eyes upon her even as she walked off down the gleaming corridor, fighting to make her legs work the way they were meant to do. To keep herself upright. Not to slump against the nearest wall the way she wanted to.

Shona didn't think she pulled in a full breath until she rounded the corner.

She had learned her way around the palace in these weeks she'd been trapped here, but that didn't make it feel any more familiar to her. She wasn't certain she could ever really get used to all the luxury on conspicuous display at every turn. The marble. The gold. Statues and fine art in every alcove. Mosaics on the floors and the walls.

It was exactly what a palace ought to be, she supposed—but it wasn't home.

It wasn't *her* home.

Shona stopped next to one of the fountains and dipped her fingers into the cool water. Far above, the ceiling opened up to let in the night, and the moon was silvery as it danced down into the water.

She wanted to cry.

She knew there were eyes on her regardless of whether she could see them or not. Everywhere she went, everything she did, she was watched. Gossiped about. Discussed and dissected. Her advisors had made that clear to her every day, in case she hadn't noticed it on her own as she'd tried to go about her business here, such as it was. The simple truth of the matter was that Shona no longer belonged to herself. Whether she decided to become Malak's queen—assuming that was a decision she was even allowed to make, of course, and wasn't simply tossed a crown and made to wear it—or refused, she would always be tied to this place. These people.

Because Miles was.

That had been bad enough. That unpleasant realization that never seemed to get easier no matter how many times she told herself to get over it. To accept it. To move on from the things she couldn't change, because to do anything else was to ask to feel crazy. And to set herself up for more of the same.

Miles was Malak's son. If she left here tomorrow, that wouldn't change. And little as she might like to think about it, that simple truth meant that Miles would always belong here. One day he would rule this kingdom as surely as his father did.

She didn't have to like it. It didn't matter if she liked it. It was the truth either way.

It was one thing to have her son used against her.

It was something else entirely to have her body used in the exact same manner.

Whether she liked it or not, her own cries seemed to echo in her ears. There was no sound in the atrium where she stood save the splashing of the water, but still, all she heard was her own voice. Her own loss of control.

Her total and complete surrender.

She sat on the lip of the fountain and moved her fingers through the water. This way, then that. She stared fiercely at the place where the fountain met the pool beneath it, hoping that would keep her own tears from falling.

And in her head, all she could hear—all she could see—was what had happened on Malak's balcony.

She could still see him kneeling down before her, his wide shoulders keeping her legs apart and his hard hands holding her hips where he wanted them.

His mouth against the part of her that yearned the most.

Out here in this atrium, all by herself, she was still slick. Melting hot.

And ashamed of herself.

She didn't know how long she sat there. It could have been moments or hours.

But she heard the scuff of a foot against the marble behind her before she heard a voice. The same voice she always heard.

"Mistress?" Yadira called from the shadows that lined the atrium. "Are you unwell?"

Someone had seen her, no doubt, and reported back to Yadira that Shona was not where she was supposed to be. Because somebody would always pass on something like that. Because there was no hiding here, in this palace that appeared so vast.

There was no hiding anywhere.

Not even from herself.

"I'm fine," she said, and rose to her feet. Her

legs still felt like jelly, but she didn't let that slow her down. She ignored it as she walked toward the woman who was more her jailer than her servant, and she even got herself to smile as she did it. "It's a beautiful night, isn't it?"

She tuned out Yadira's usual chatter as they walked back across the palace to Shona's own suite of rooms. She nodded her thanks and smiled her way into her bedroom, where she took a long, hot shower and then crawled into her bed at last.

Because it was only there, in the dark of her bedroom with the covers pulled high over her head, that she could allow her face to crumple as it would. It was only there that she could permit her tears to fall, that she could face the fact that the worst part of what had happened with Malak tonight—and that night five years ago—was that she'd wanted it.

She'd more than wanted it. She'd longed for it.

And she'd loved every wicked pass of his tongue against the softest part of her.

So much that she still ached, well into the night, even as she was lying there alone and beating herself up for betraying every last thing she'd thought she stood for.

And worse, she had no idea what it said about her that she should want the man she knew would be the end of her, one way or another.

Or what to do now that he knew it.

* * *

Malak wasn't the least bit surprised the following night when Shona stayed in her seat after the nannies took away Miles.

"Do you not wish to take your normal stance of pointless defiance?" He leaned back against his pillows and studied her as she glared at him. "I was hoping for another decadent dessert tonight, I must tell you. This is a disappointment."

She looked different tonight, he thought. Not exactly subdued, but…contained.

As if he wasn't the only one who had come to some conclusions about this little war of theirs.

"I prefer to sit," she said after a moment. She even smiled, though Malak would scarcely call it polite. It was a pretense for her to be so civil. "But thank you."

"Are you certain? I so enjoyed the last time you stood before me. I know you would not dare to tell me you did not."

"Congratulations," she said, that dark gaze of hers meeting his in that steady, challenging manner no one else would dare. "You won that battle, I guess. You got me to sit down. But what else have you really gained?"

Malak grinned. "You mean, aside from the sheer joy of your sweet little—"

"Sex doesn't change anything," she said, cutting him off. And he had to stop registering surprise every time she did things no one else would dream of doing in his presence. Much less *to* him. "It's just sex. It doesn't change the fact that I don't want to be here. That I don't want to be a queen at all, and certainly not *your* queen. That I have no interest in any of this."

Maybe it was the fact that she didn't seem particularly angry about it that allowed him to consider her objections to all of this a little more carefully than he had before. Or maybe it was that he'd tasted her again and had spent a night plagued by dreams of all the things he could have done had he not left her on that balcony.

After all, it was hard to maintain any level of reasonable fury when all he wanted was another taste.

Either way, he considered her for a long moment. "I assure you, you are not the only one whose wishes were not consulted in this. If that makes you feel any better."

He could see from the expression that flitted over her face that it did not. But she didn't throw that back at him as she sat there on the other side of the low table, her hands in her lap. Malak found himself mesmerized by the elegant curve of her neck, and only partly because he'd had his mouth there the night before and knew—now and again and always—how she tasted. Tonight she had her hair pulled up into something complicated, her tight curls bound together on top of her head, spilling this way and that.

Every time he saw her she was more beautiful. Malak didn't understand how that was possible, only that it was true.

"Surely you always knew that you might be king," Shona said, frowning at him as if he'd lied to her. Another insult he chose to ignore.

"Not at all." Malak made himself smile. Lazily and easily, the way his life had been until recent months had changed everything. "I was the spare. My older brother, Zufar, was meant to be king and he has been trained since his birth to take over the role. My sister, Galila, and I were both afterthoughts in our own ways."

He didn't mention his high-strung, selfish mother's indiscretions, and only partly because he was still coming to terms with them himself. To say nothing of that half brother he still didn't quite know how to make sense of. Especially since Adir's existence made Malak's life make a different sort of sense. His mother had chosen to have the baby of the man she'd loved, then had given Adir away. Malak was the child she'd dutifully had and had never loved. The way he'd been ignored all these years made a painful sort of sense, really.

He didn't mention his mother's death, or the way his father's encompassing grief over her loss brought back entirely too many memories of the way his father had ignored his children all their lives—the better to cater to a woman who had never

cared for him in return. His father had abdicated his
throne out of grief. His brother had then followed
in his footsteps and abdicated for love. Malak understood neither of these choices, but he didn't have
to understand. He only had to play his prescribed
role and do his duty.

"My sister was more of a pampered, special toy
to my parents, at least until she grew older and my
mother viewed her as competition," Malak said, because he didn't mind Shona knowing these things.
She would hear them all soon enough, once the palace gossips decided to share their stories with her
instead of just talking about her. "But I was completely ignored, always. A state of affairs that suited
me just fine, to be clear. I've never wanted to play a
starring role in my family's many storms." He forced
his smile to deepen and waved a hand, encompassing the palace, the kingdom. "And yet I was caught
up in them all the same."

Shona frowned. "But surely the purpose of a spare
is always to step in at a moment's notice."

"Theoretically, of course it is. But no one could
have anticipated that my brother would abdicate.
Least of all my brother."

"Why did he?"

Malak's smile felt fiercer than usual then, even
on his own mouth. "It appears the downfall of the
men in my family is love. It ruins them all, sooner
or later."

Shona's gaze met his and he hated, suddenly, that he couldn't read her. "'Them?'"

She didn't say "but not you." Yet still it seemed to hang there between them.

And that wasn't the only thing that shimmered in that space.

"I believe in sex, Shona," he told her, because if he couldn't make it better, he wanted to make it worse. "It might not change anything, as you said, but that's never how it feels. I believe in hot nights that ache forever, and shave off parts of your soul in return for all that pleasure. But that is all I believe in. You don't need to concern yourself that I'll ever pretend that sex is anything more than exactly what it is."

"Of course you believe in sex, but never, ever love." Shona shook her head at him as if he was... silly. Or a small child. He had to grit his teeth to keep himself from reacting to both insults the way he would have liked to. "Isn't that a hallmark of men like you?"

"I beg your pardon. Are there men like me? Anywhere? I rather doubt it."

"I've never heard of a man alive who imagines that he is capable of love, even if the only thing he is king of is his own living-room couch." Shona's gaze was entirely too steady on his, as if she meant to indict him with every arch, deceptively soft syllable she uttered. He assumed she did. "My understanding has always been that the world might end if a single man ever imagined himself capable of such a thing. And yet here we all are."

Malak laughed at that. Because it was that or reach for her again, and he didn't want to cede his advantage. "The difference between the vast phalanxes of men you apparently know so well, aside from the obvious fact that I am the ruler of an entire country rather than a piece of furniture, is that I know myself."

He didn't tell her what else he knew. All the ways that love had ruined his father, for example. And all the rest of them, caught up as they were in the wreckage of their parents' sad little marriage. He had always known that such excesses of emotion were not for him. That he would never fall, not like his father had. He would never let the love of a woman blind him to the rest of his life.

Especially not when there were so many other, more entertaining excesses to explore.

That was how he'd lived his life, until these past months.

It wasn't that he thought he was immune to love, because he wasn't. He loved his family. He loved his country. He felt fairly certain that the epic punch he'd felt at the first sight of Miles was love, too—one that grew the more time he spent with the boy.

But he had absolutely no intention of wrecking himself over a woman the way his father had. And was still doing after that woman's death. That the woman in question was his own mother didn't make Malak any more kindly disposed toward his father's complete loss of himself.

Malak had never expected to take his father's or brother's place. But now that he had, he did not intend to follow in their footsteps and make their same mistakes.

He had vowed to himself that whatever else happened, he never would.

"If you say so," Shona said, and she didn't even sound particularly dismissive. But then, she didn't have to. It was written all over her.

And Malak didn't understand how he had gone from being completely at his ease to…this. He didn't know what to call that churning sensation inside of him, as if his skin had suddenly grown too tight and nothing inside of him could bear it.

"I not only know myself, I know you," he told her, because he felt weaponless, suddenly, and he couldn't allow it.

She didn't laugh, though her dark eyes filled with a kind of mirth. "You don't know anything about me. Thank God."

"But I do, Shona." He shook his head at her, regaining his equilibrium as he did. "Do you imagine that I would allow just any woman to walk in off the streets and take her place at my side? Without knowing every possible detail about her?"

"If she was unlucky enough to have found herself pregnant with your child, yes. Absolutely. I think anyone would do."

Malak didn't like the way she said that. Especially because she wasn't wrong.

And he didn't know why he felt as if he had something to prove, suddenly. Or possibly it was more about regaining the upper hand. He wasn't precisely proud of that urge—but that didn't diminish it.

"I know more about you than you might imagine," he told her. "I know that you spent the first part of your life in the foster system. Is that not what they call it in America when you are taken into the care of the state?"

"I don't hide the fact that I was in foster care. That's not exactly a secret."

"I imagine we can trace your foolhardy stubbornness and unnecessary independence to that experience."

"Or, perhaps, to me simply being an actual adult. Who, like most actual adults, doesn't like being bullied by strange men."

"Yes, *men*. You know so much about them, you tell me. You have a great many philosophies. And yet my investigators were unable to come up with the slightest shred of evidence that you've ever touched one." He smiled. "Aside from me, of course."

She studied him for a moment. "Does that make you feel special?"

But before he could answer, she laughed. And Malak did not like the way she laughed. And kept laughing, as if he'd told a marvelous joke. She even wiped at her eyes, as if she'd laughed so hard she'd made herself cry.

"I had a baby, Malak. And not in a palace like this. There were no packs of nannies roaming about the streets of New Orleans, desperate for the opportunity to give me a hand. Even if I'd wanted to date somebody, I had no time. And I definitely didn't have any energy." She shook her head at him. "Besides, the experience of having a one-night stand and being left pregnant and alone to handle the consequences was somehow less entertaining than you seem to imagine. Why would I want to repeat it?"

"This confirms what I thought," Malak said after a moment. "Last night in particular. You don't know."

He could feel the tension in the air between them. But he knew, now, it wasn't the way she looked at him. It wasn't the lies he imagined she told herself to explain it all away. Perhaps she took solace in them.

But the truth was, she didn't know.

"What don't I know?" Shona asked, in the tone of one who would have much preferred not to ask the question at all.

Malak thought about her taste. Her scent. The sweetness that was only hers and that he wanted almost more than he could bear. "You don't know that this isn't normal. This thing between us. You think this happens all the time."

She laughed again, though he thought it sounded far more uneasy than before. "I was under the impression that for you, it did."

"Sex, Shona. Sex is easy enough. But this?"

He leaned forward then and stretched his hand across the table. He saw her jolt, as if she meant to pull away but then ordered herself to remain still, to fight some more, because that was what she did—what they did, if he was honest. He reached over and took one of her hands in his. That was all.

But it was enough.

"This," he told her softly, as wildfire arced between them. The sizzle. The burn. "This is in no way *usual*, my fierce little queen."

Shona stared at him, her gaze too dark to read.

"Careful," she said quietly. "You wouldn't want someone to think you were falling in love, would you? Not after all the bold statements you made." She tilted her head to one side. "My little king."

Malak didn't like any part of what she'd said. Not the absurd mention of love when he'd already told her he was immune, or the insulting endearment he was sure she knew was offensive. But he would be damned if he'd let her see that. Any of that.

He didn't have it in him to ruin himself the way the rest of his family had.

He refused.

"You don't need to worry about whether I might fall," he said, somehow keeping his temper in check. He imagined it had something to do with the wildfire greed that coursed through him, making him hard. Making him as close to desperate as he'd ever been. "Better by far you should worry about yourself."

"I'm not worried about me at all." That belligerent chin of hers lifted. "Are you?"

"I want you in my bed," he told her, and watched that molten heat make her eyes go glassy again, just the way he liked them. "I'm tired of this game. There is no escaping this marriage or this throne, and I regret to inform you that you are stuck in it as surely as I am. But what I don't understand is why you want to fight when you know how good it is between us."

"You're talking about sex," she bit out, though her voice was hoarse. "That's not a marriage."

His hand gripped hers tighter when she tried to pull it away. "It's the best part of a marriage. And the only part I have any interest in, if I am honest."

"Marriage is more than stunts out on balconies," she threw at him, her voice stronger. And this time, when she pulled her hand away, he let her. "It's about sharing your life. It's not about threatening someone with their own child. It's not about battles for custody and kidnap attempts. It's supposed to be a partnership."

He bared his teeth. "What do you know about marriage?"

"Nothing," she threw at him, as if this was another battle. But he thought she sounded desperate, as if she feared she was losing it. "Nothing at all, except that I don't want to marry you. I don't."

And this time, when she stood up and made as if to walk from the room, Malak concentrated on her desperation, that suggested he'd already won, and let her go.

CHAPTER SEVEN

SOME DAYS LATER, Shona was escorted back to her rooms in the middle of the day when she would normally have expected to be corralled somewhere with another set of dour royal advisors for more tedious lessons about the role she resolutely declined the opportunity to play.

"What's going on?" she asked Yadira drily when she was delivered to her own sitting room and found the other woman waiting for her. "Am I finally getting a little bit of built-in naptime in between all these exhausting stonewalling episodes?"

Yadira smiled in that way she did that told Shona that her personal servant—a term Shona still didn't care for on any level—didn't think much of her witticisms. And maybe there really, truly was something wrong with Shona. Because the less the people in the palace seemed to find her amusing, up to and including the king, the more she kept right on doing the very thing it was they found so distasteful. Over and over and over again.

She was beginning to think that she was naturally perverse. Or something worse. Something a little closer to *boneheaded*, another familiar term she'd been called by various foster parents.

"I have laid out clothes for you, mistress," Yadira said in her deliberately calm manner that Shona understood was her own form of a weapon—and one she aimed well, every time.

"I think you can see that I'm already dressed."

"Indeed. But the king has specifically requested that you wear what has been chosen for you today."

"I was under the impression that the king made the same request every morning." Shona eyed the other woman, who stood there emanating a kind of wholesale meekness Shona was beginning to suspect she didn't actually possess. "Has that been you, all along?"

"Shona."

She didn't have to turn to identify that voice. She would know it anywhere. It haunted her dreams in ways she pretended she couldn't remember every morning when she woke up, heart pounding with an ache between her legs.

But she had never heard Malak's voice *here* before. Here in this suite of rooms that she had, perhaps foolishly, begun to view as her refuge. The one place in the palace she could escape this crazy new life she'd been hauled into, at least for a little bit.

And better still, where she could escape from him.

"FAST FIVE" READER SURVEY

Your participation entitles you to:
✳ 4 Thank-You Gifts Worth Over $20!

Complete the survey in minutes.

Get 2 FREE Books

See inside for details.

Dear Reader,

Since you are a lover of our books, your opinions are important to us... and so is your time.

That's why we made sure your **"FAST FIVE" READER SURVEY** can be completed in just a few minutes. Your answers to the five questions will help us remain at the forefront of women's fiction.

And, as a thank-you for participating, we'd like to send you **4 FREE THANK-YOU GIFTS!**

Enjoy your gifts with our appreciation,

Pam Powers

To get your
4 FREE THANK-YOU GIFTS:

✳ Quickly complete the "Fast Five" Reader Survey
and return the insert.

"FAST FIVE" READER SURVEY

1 Do you sometimes read a book a second or third time? ○ Yes ○ No

2 Do you often choose reading over other forms of entertainment such as television? ○ Yes ○ No

3 When you were a child, did someone regularly read aloud to you? ○ Yes ○ No

4 Do you sometimes take a book with you when you travel outside the home? ○ Yes ○ No

5 In addition to books, do you regularly read newspapers and magazines? ○ Yes ○ No

YES! I have completed the above Reader Survey. Please send me my 4 FREE GIFTS (gifts worth over $20 retail). I understand that I am under no obligation to buy anything, as explained on the back of this card.

❏ I prefer the regular-print edition
106/306 HDL GM3S

❏ I prefer the larger-print edition
176/376 HDL GM3S

FIRST NAME   LAST NAME

ADDRESS

APT.#   CITY

STATE/PROV.   ZIP/POSTAL CODE

P-817-FF18

READER SERVICE—Here's how it works:

◄ If offer card is missing write to: Reader Service, P.O. Box 1341, Buffalo, NY 14240-8531 or visit www.ReaderService.com ◄

BUSINESS REPLY MAIL
FIRST-CLASS MAIL   PERMIT NO. 717   BUFFALO, NY

POSTAGE WILL BE PAID BY ADDRESSEE

READER SERVICE
PO BOX 1341
BUFFALO NY 14240-8571

NO POSTAGE
NECESSARY
IF MAILED
IN THE
UNITED STATES

"I'm sorry," she said, keeping her gaze on Yadira. "I thought these were my private rooms."

"I think you will find it is my palace," Malak said.

Shona didn't want to look at him. But she made herself do it anyway because what she wanted even less than a glimpse of him was to show any hint of weakness. Particularly in front of Yadira.

"Forgive me," she said, and she was proud of how steady her voice was. "I'm only emotionally prepared to see you at dinnertime. This is...alarming, to say the least."

"There is no need to be alarmed."

"And if I was truly, deeply alarmed, your telling me not to be would change it...how, exactly?"

Malak's dark green eyes flashed, but he ignored that. "There is a small ceremony taking place shortly. Your presence is required. And I'm afraid that it will be recorded for posterity, so you must dress according to expectations. *My* expectations, before you ask."

"I thought we had discussed your expectations already."

His mouth curved. "But in this case, my expectations are not my problem—they instead carry the weight of the whole kingdom. It is unavoidable, I'm afraid. You might as well resign yourself to that now."

There was a kind of disconcerting steel in the way

he gazed at her, and it occurred to Shona that there could be only one reason that he had actually come all the way over to this side of the palace. And was actually standing here, personally demanding she dress in a certain way. She glanced at Yadira, then back at Malak, but could read nothing on either one of their faces.

"Are you here to force me into some awful costume?"

"I don't like that word. I am the king of Khalia, am I not? Surely I need only make a request for my will to be done. Force is quite beneath me."

"I know we've covered this. You're not *my* king."

She heard Yadira's shocked gasp, but what really bothered her was the fact that she felt a kick of shame along with it. As if she'd agreed, somewhere or somehow, to keep her fight with Malak to herself, when she knew very well she'd done no such thing.

His gaze was steady on hers, and she didn't know why that made it worse. Only that it did.

"It is always such a delight to have these arguments with you, Shona, particularly when they inevitably end my way." He didn't look delighted. But he didn't look particularly affronted, either. And Shona was starting to view that veneer of laziness he liked to cloak himself in with suspicion. "But there is no time for the game today. I'm afraid this is a matter of some urgency and importance, or I would, of course, continue to support your curious need to wear and rewear the least attractive items of clothing in your wardrobe. And stand through dinners. And ignore your tutors. And all your other pointless attempts at defiance."

"There is no way—"

"Shona." And with that, he flipped a switch. She could see it just as easily as she could hear it in his voice. She felt her spine straighten against her will. "This is not about you. This is not about any battle you seem to feel you need to keep fighting with me. This is about Miles."

She swallowed, though it was harder than it should have been. "Miles doesn't care how I dress."

"I am certain he does not," Malak said coolly. "But we are discussing my official coronation and what will happen there. Miles will be introduced as my son and heir, the crown prince to the throne of Khalia. This will be his first introduction to the kingdom and, more than that, to the world. Do you really want every eye to focus on you and the inappropriateness of your outfit? Is that what you want them to take away from their first exposure to your son?"

Her heart seemed to squeeze too tight at that question. As if she was actively failing her child when none of this was what she'd wanted in the first place.

"I didn't agree to this. I didn't agree to any parading of Miles in front of—"

"I have put this off for as long as I could already," Malak said, still in that implacable way of his that made her fight to keep from showing her reaction. "It cannot be put off any longer. Miles is here now. He is happy. I cannot imagine he will view a stuffy, private ceremony any differently than he would one of his usual adventures in the palace. The worry is not Miles, Shona. It's you."

That bit of shame she'd felt before bloomed wider. Deeper and hotter. She sucked in a breath, amazed that something like this could get to her. Surely she shouldn't care. Surely she should be sure enough of herself and who she was to scoff at the notion that the clothing she wore might make any kind of difference to her child.

Not your child, a voice inside said in a similarly implacable manner. *But his prospects, his future.*

And that was worse. That hurt more.

"You're presenting him to your kingdom as your crown prince," she said quietly, because there was no use arguing that he wasn't just as happy and well-adjusted here as Malak had said he was. And it didn't matter how she felt about that, or the fact that her baby had a role to play in this place whether she liked it or not. "You don't need me there. What I wear while out of public view shouldn't matter at all."

Malak looked past her for a moment and did something with one eyebrow that sent Yadira hurrying from the room. Then he returned that imperious gaze of his to Shona.

"I have been patient with you," he told her, though there was no evidence of that patience in his tone, then. Much less in his glittering dark green eyes. "You can spend every night between now and eternity arguing with me in the privacy of my rooms, if you wish. I welcome it. Perhaps I even crave it, since it is the only remnant I have left of the carefree life I will never have again, one in which people talk to me as if I do not have the power to end their lives with the click of my fingers."

Shona swallowed. "Is that a threat?"

"I have allowed you to keep reality at bay too long, clearly. Is this really so much to ask, Shona? There is a certain way the mother of the crown prince of Khalia must look. Act. It is not to put you in a box or whatever your objection to it is today. It is to protect *him*. I am starting to believe it is not that you don't see the truth of that, but that you do not want to see it."

"Miles doesn't care how I dress," she said again. And more fiercely this time. "What I wear has absolutely nothing to do with him or the role you want him to play for you."

"I wish that were so," Malak replied, all ice and certainty. "Perhaps it is true where you come from, but this is Khalia. There are expectations of royal behavior, whether we like it or not. And the tragedy

for you is that I have spent my life ignoring those
expectations. I was a playboy. I was a disappointment. I was everyone's favorite scandal without even
trying. I reveled in the fact that I could be depended
upon to horrify the good people of this kingdom
without even rising from my bed in the morning,
because it is all fun and games when there is no
possibility that you might ever ascend the throne.
But now I have."

"My condolences," Shona gritted out.

"What it means, sadly, is that everything I touch,
everything going forward, must be excruciatingly
correct to make up for all my misbehavior."

"You seem to be under the impression that your
life and your problems are somehow mine, too." Her
voice felt strangled in her own throat. Her chest felt
much too tight, as if she might crack in two at any
moment.

"What is it you want, Shona?" Malak demanded
then, and though there was fire in that gaze of his,
his voice was cold. "You do not want to be queen.
You do not want to take on board even the small-
est lesson my people try to teach you about how
best to fit in here. You do not want to learn a single
thing that might help you feel more comfortable in
this world. You would prefer to stalk about the palace, scowling at everyone, making certain that even
the lowliest maid knows full well you do not belong
here and never will. Is that it? Is that truly what you

want? Because you are already well on your way to achieving it, if so."

That it was such an accurate description of her behavior over the past few weeks stung. But more than that, it was an apt description of her behavior in every foster home Shona had ever been thrown into.

And that rocked her.

Had nothing changed at all? She'd been out of the foster system for eight years, and a mother for four. Had she learned nothing in all that time? Was she still that same surly teenage girl, well aware that no one would ever happen along and adopt her at her age, and was therefore determined to push everyone away before they could do the same to her? Or worse?

It made her feel sick. It made her feel unsteady on her own feet.

It made her want to take a swing at the man who stood before her, so easily shredding her to pieces. He'd done it that night on his balcony. He did it, again and again, as she sat at his table. And now this.

She wanted to open her mouth and admit it. She wanted to act like the grown woman she'd fought so hard to become, for a change, not that eternally passed-over foster kid who hadn't mattered to anyone. But she couldn't do it. She couldn't give away the only weapon she'd ever had, no matter that every time she used it she was really only hurting herself.

But she didn't know how to stop.

"Every single thing that's happened since you set foot in that restaurant in New Orleans has been about you," she said instead, and she kept her gaze steady on him as if that could make her steady, too. As if it could change that rocking, rolling sensation beneath her feet. "Your life. Your kingdom. Your throne. Your son. You, you, you. And I get it. You're the king, as you'll be the first to remind me." She found one fist over her heart and pressed it in, deep. "But I have my own life. And guess what? I have my own dreams. My own hopes. My own—"

"Wonderful," he interrupted, in that same harsh tone. He moved closer to her, towering over her in a manner she should have found intimidating. But she didn't. She felt…melty and too soft and lit on fire, but not intimidated. "Tell me your dreams, Shona. I will make them come true. This is what I do."

"I want to be free," she shot back at him.

He didn't laugh. Not exactly, though he made a sound that could have been something like it. Only devoid of any humor.

"What does that mean to you?" he asked. "You throw that word around, but tell me, what would you do with this freedom you are so obsessed with?"

Shona glared up at him. "Live my life without all this commentary on my wardrobe, for one thing."

Malak didn't take that bait. "Will you head back to that restaurant in New Orleans? Will you toil away at your two jobs and never quite make ends meet? Fight to pay the rent on a disgraceful house in that appalling neighborhood? You've been free to live out your dreams for the past four years. And what have you done with it?"

Shona pressed her curled fingers harder against her rib cage and told herself she wasn't shaking, deep inside. "I've raised your crown prince. You're welcome, by the way."

"And what else?" An expression she couldn't identify moved over his face when she didn't answer him immediately, that on another man she might have called something like desperate. But this was Malak. "This is not a test. I want to know. You've spent nearly a month here, and in all that time, all you have told me is what you are not. You are not this person or that person. You will not do this, you will not do that. What do you *want*, Shona?"

It was another hit. A wallop, just like before, but she weathered it. Somehow she kept herself from crumbling. "I don't need to prove myself to you."

"You are so focused on what you think has been taken from you that you cannot seem to see what's been given to you." He shook his head. "You call this palace a prison, but what you fail to see is that it gives you access."

"Access to what? You?" She scoffed. "I had more than enough access to you in a hotel bar in New Orleans."

"To the world, Shona. To anything you like." He rubbed a hand over his face, and that startled her. It seemed such a perfect expression of frustration and she was amazed that she had the power to get to him when he seemed like such an impassable wall to her. She wasn't sure she liked it. "My child is by definition an extraordinarily wealthy individual. As am I. And there is no possibility that I will permit that child's mother to live in squalor. Your old life was hard, I grant you. And I admire the fact that you made it work at all. But all that hardship is a thing of the past now. Your days of working around the clock, worrying over child care and trading shifts with friends are over. You are the only one who does not seem to realize that."

Her heart was pounding. She realized she was holding her breath and forced herself to let it out.

Malak pressed his advantage. "Don't you understand? You are mine now. There are no longer any boundaries on what you can or cannot do."

"Except you. Except your boundaries."

This time, that curve to his hard, beautiful mouth seemed sad. "And this is what you think of me, in the end. That I am indistinguishable from poverty, from prison."

She didn't think that. Of course she didn't think that.

But she hated—or maybe the real truth was that she feared—that part of her that longed to reach out to him. To apologize for saying such a thing. To make him feel better, somehow, when she was still fighting off that shaking deep inside.

She bit her own tongue so hard she tasted copper.

And when she didn't speak, Malak continued in that same low, dark way that was only making her internal trembling worse.

"If you want to live out your days in this narrow, dark cage you seem to think is your only option, you are welcome to do so," he said. His tone lanced through her like some kind of terrible lightning. It made her want to defend herself. Cry. Rip herself open and bring a different version of herself out into the light, free of all the ugly weight of her childhood—but she didn't. She couldn't. She didn't know how. "But I would hope that you have better dreams for your child. He deserves better than that same small cage, do you not agree?"

He didn't wait for her to answer. He looked past her yet again, and nodded his head, and then Yadira was there again.

"Come, mistress," she said, her own voice subdued, as if everybody despaired of Shona. Including Shona herself, it seemed. "At the very least we can try on the clothes, yes?"

And Shona let the other woman take her by the elbow and steer her toward the doorway that led farther into the suite, and on toward her bedroom. She let Yadira guide her, but she couldn't seem to tear her gaze from Malak's until the very last moment. She couldn't seem to find her voice, either.

As if he had one hand around her throat.

And worse by far, the other clenched tight around her heart.

CHAPTER EIGHT

THE CORONATION CEREMONY went off smoothly. Far better than anyone, including Malak, could have hoped after the surprise of his ascension and the even bigger shock of Miles's existence. He was fairly certain his top ministers had expected something along the lines of an American reality show.

But Malak had opted instead for a private, deliberately quiet affair, because he thought it was important that Khalia's second major transfer of power in the past few months seemed so smooth it hardly merited any publicity—aside, of course, from what the papers might say about it.

Besides, he had other plans for grand, sweeping public ceremonies.

A coronation was a ritual steeped in age-old tradition of a far more prosaic sort—the consolidation of authority into a single man. Less myth, more might. Malak had planned his down to the barest, most minute detail, because he wanted the somber images he planned to release to live in his people's heads and hearts as if they had always been there.

Malak himself, looking quietly authoritative, accepted his place on the ancient throne in traditional Khalian dress. The ritual naming of his heir, that he knew would inspire his people to raptures. For who could resist tiny, fierce-faced Miles, staring up at his father with an identical look of concentration in those same dark green eyes?

And everything went as it should. Precisely as Malak had planned.

Except for Shona.

She had disappeared into her room with her servant earlier, looking shaken. Malak had found he didn't like it. He preferred Shona bright and ferocious, not quietly obedient—though he hardly knew where to put such a thought after all the effort he'd expended attempting to break her even a little. And then she had emerged again some time later dressed appropriately for her station.

At last.

And he'd forgotten what he liked or didn't like about her emotional state, because he was, after all, just a man.

And she was so gorgeous it made his lungs hurt.

Malak had gone to significant trouble to find the perfect dress that encompassed both the sort of Western chic that would broadcast Shona's beauty to the whole world and the suggestion of the kind of modesty his people would expect from a woman who had already borne him a son and would soon take her place at his side.

And she had exceeded his wildest expectations.

Shona was always beautiful. But it had never occurred to him how much she tried to hide that. With her aloofness. With her toughness. With her refusal to back down, ever, even so much as an inch. It wasn't simply the way she dressed, it was how she carried herself.

As if she dared any man, even him, to find her beautiful when she could be a thorn in the side instead.

But it was as if the dress brought out a different side of her. A Shona he'd never met before, this one as soft as she was determined. No longer disguising her stunning beauty, but owning it at long last.

"Are you satisfied?" she'd asked him when she stood there, her hair a gorgeous dark halo around her and her brown eyes fixed on his while the dark green dress managed to both hide and celebrate her figure in a rush and tumble toward the floor.

And at any other time, that would have been a challenge. But not today.

Today, Malak had thought, she actually wanted to know his answer. Did he dare imagine she wanted his approval?

"I am completely satisfied," he'd told her, though

his voice was more gravelly than it should have been and his head was in the gutter.

It was harder than it should have been to simply extend his arm to her. Not to put his hands on her. Not to take her back into that bedroom and explore this new, even more stunning version of Shona with every part of his own exultant, needy body.

Not to call her what she was. *His queen.*

Instead, after a slight hesitation, she'd taken his arm. And she'd let him lead her through the palace.

"All you have to do is stand with Miles, smile a bit and look reasonably pleased to be involved in something of such import. Can you do that?" he had asked her as he'd walked them both toward the throne room his great grandfather had built for the express purpose of awing peasants and visitors alike.

His earlier ancestors had never seen a need for such a thing. They'd ruled by might and guile through the strength of their armies and the sheer audacity of their military strategies out here in these treacherous deserts. Thrones and crowns had been secondary, little more than affectations and fripperies to hardened warrior kings who took what they wanted and held it by the force of their will alone.

And somewhere between the power of his ancestors and the spectacle of modernity, Malak needed to find his own way to rule.

It made him…uneasy, almost, to consider how

little he could imagine holding this throne without Shona. When had that happened? They had been forced back together because of a long-ago mistake and he should have hated that. He *had* hated the very idea of it, once upon a time. He was sure he had.

He didn't understand why he didn't hate it anymore. Why *hate* wasn't at all the word he'd use to describe the situation he found himself in with this woman.

Not that he would allow it to be anything else.

"I will do my best," she had replied. She'd shot him a look, holding herself very straight and tall as if some of those comportment classes had sunk in, after all. "For Miles's sake."

And Malak could hardly complain that she was hiding behind Miles when he had used his son to the same purpose himself. But it chafed at him.

And as he'd gone about his sacred duty, promising himself to his kingdom and his people, mouthing ancient words he had never thought would be his to say aloud, he found himself thinking less about the awesome responsibilities before him and more about this woman who still didn't seem to realize she was destined to be his queen.

When there could be no other outcome.

And if he was honest, only a very small part of that had to do with the son they shared.

Afterward, in the small, formal reception that

was filled with palace advisors and a host of his ministers, only a portion of his attention was on the usual political machinations, jostling for position and naked ambition amongst his courtiers. What he was focused on was Shona.

Shona, who kept a mysterious half smile on her face as she stood slightly off to one side, Miles there in front of her with his eyes wide. Shona, who gazed down at her son with that fierce pride written all over her—and the strangest thing was how Malak shared it. He could feel it in him, too. Miles had been outfitted to look like the miniature version of his father he was, and something about that made Malak's chest ache.

But then, all of this did. The three of them standing together like this *did something* to him. He'd gotten good at ignoring it during the dinners they shared, but today it seemed less like a vague ache and more like a pulled tendon, sharp and inescapable, no matter how he stood or tried to catch his breath.

He could see how they'd look in all the pictures they'd taken today. Malak and Shona with Miles between them. Miles a few shades darker than Malak's own brown skin and a few shades lighter than his mother. Like the happy family Malak had never known himself. The kind of happy family he'd never believed in.

A perfect set, something in him whispered.

When the nannies came to lead Miles away, Shona made as if to go with him, but Malak stopped her.

"I thought I would—"

"Remain behind with your lord and king?" Malak smiled at her frozen expression. "What an excellent idea."

And he knew he'd gotten through to her somehow, because she made no move to create the sort of scene he knew full well she could have done, if she wished. And would have done a week ago. Possibly even yesterday. Instead, she stood with quiet dignity at his elbow, and stayed with him as he finished all his official conversations.

Malak doubted she knew that she had as good as announced her intention to wed him to every minister and courtier in the palace. And every subject of his who would see their pictures in the papers. But he knew.

And it felt a great deal like triumph—which he, in turn, enjoyed a whole lot more than all those other things he'd have preferred not to feel.

"Your ministers can't possibly think that was appropriate," she said when they were alone again, the last two in the formal hall outside the throne room. Malak loosened the tie of the very exquisitely cut Western suit he'd worn for the reception.

"If you mean the fact that I am dressed more like a Western king than the sheikh I am in my bones and my blood, believe me, there were many complaints."

He eyed her as if she'd made them. "But none I listened to, as you can see."

Shona blinked. "What's wrong with how you're dressed?"

And then she looked flustered, as if the question revealed more than she'd meant it to.

Malak didn't try very hard to hide his smile. "Nothing at all if the throne I wished to ascend was in Europe. Didn't you hear the questions the reporter asked about that very thing?"

Shona was standing in the middle of the room, a vision in that formal dress that looked even better on her than Malak had imagined it would. She stood straight and almost too still, as if she was afraid to move. As if the wrong breath might lead to something far worse than the sudden intimacy of being the only two remaining in a formally crowded room.

"It's very difficult to listen to so many people talk at once," she said after a moment. "The reporter, the interpreter and then you as you answered."

"Which is why you should take Arabic lessons," he replied mildly, and smiled when her gaze cut to his with more of the heat he was used to. "It cuts down on the chatter. Alas, the tutor I hired for you tells me that you have yet to sit through a single one of her carefully crafted—"

"You made your point earlier." Her dark eyes glittered as she looked at him. "You don't have to beat me over the head with it. And no, I didn't hear the interpreter say anything about your clothes."

"I wore traditional dress in the throne room and Western dress to the reception, upending centuries of tradition and, according to some, betraying my crass soul for all to see. Because I wish to straddle both worlds. I intend to be a progressive king."

"Progressive?" she echoed. In clear disbelief. "You?"

"Indeed. There are parts of this kingdom that have remained unchanged since the twelfth century. Villages that have yet to enter the bold new world of the thirteenth century, much less the twenty-first."

"But…progressive?" She let out a sound that was close enough to a laugh to make his eyes narrow. "That is not a word I would use to describe you."

"My politics are considered remarkably progressive, in fact," he assured her. "Here in Khalia, that is, where I am known as a great libertine, who wasted the better part of the last decade immersing myself in the scandalous pleasures of loose and casual Western cities and their many licentious women."

"Right. And because of that you have such a liberal view of, say, marriage."

"See?" His voice was soft. He doubted very much his expression matched. "You can do battle with me just as easily dressed like this as you can in those strange ensembles you cobbled together from the depths of your closet."

He thought she looked shaken again, but if she did, she hid it in the next moment, forcing him to contemplate, yet again, the elegant line of her neck.

"It's easy for you to say such things," Shona said softly. "You have nothing to lose."

She turned then and Malak almost let her go. But there was something about the way she moved toward the door, her head angled toward the floor and her hands in fists at her side. It caught at him. It made him question—

But that was not who he was, damn it all. That was not what he did.

He had never been a man of *what-ifs* and *maybes*. He did not *feel*. He had seen, then taken. His conquests had been legendary.

Hell, she was one of them.

Malak caught up to her in the next atrium, with a set of three fountains in the center, greenery and bright magenta flowers flowing from the pillars, and walls bedecked with a thousand tiny mirrors set into the tiles.

And he had not touched her in so long. *Too long.* It seemed like forever. He reached out and took her wrist, pulling her around to face him again.

Gently. Inexorably. And what he noticed most was how easily she came, spinning back to him as if this was some kind of dance. As if they both knew the steps. As if they shared this same gripping thing that was making his chest feel tight and the rest of him…greedy.

"What do you think you have to lose?" he asked her, and his voice sounded almost gruff. But then, perhaps it matched that arrested expression on her lovely face.

Her gaze searched his. She swallowed, and his eyes moved to track the movement. He held her so he could feel the tumult of her pulse beneath the smooth, dark brown expanse of her satiny skin. He expected her to tug her wrist from his grip, but she didn't.

Instead, she turned her head to the side and nodded toward the hundreds of mirrors on the nearest wall that together made a great, reflective pool.

"Look at that," she whispered, something fierce and yet broken in her voice. "You look like a king. You belong here, surrounded by all of this. Fountains and jewels, thrones and servants. But I look exactly like what I am. A foster kid playing dress-up."

If she'd reached into his chest and dug out his heart with those elegant fingers of hers, he couldn't have been more surprised. More taken back.

"You look like a beautiful woman, Shona. Elegant and without equal."

"Just stop." She didn't say it in her usual bitter and harsh way. It was more of a sigh. She shook her head at their reflection. "I never played princesses. Or any other games of make-believe. I'm not that kind of person. I don't need that kind of escape from reality—or anyway, I never liked it. Why pretend things are better when they'll be just as terrible on the other side of whatever game you're playing?"

She was telling him something important. Even if Malak couldn't understand it, not completely, he could feel it. It was like a shudder, working its way down his spine. It settled deep in his belly, like a kind of foreboding.

"I am not a make-believe king, little one," he told her quietly, moving there beside her, dark and tall while she was so lithe and pretty. And she fit him. Her head reached his shoulder and he wanted to turn her toward him, make her tilt up that chin, and get a taste of that proud, lush mouth that haunted his dreams. "When you become my queen, and you will, it will not be a game we play. It will be real."

He didn't understand what it was she was looking at, there on the wall in so many gleaming tiles, what she saw in their reflection that made her brown eyes look so anguished.

He wasn't surprised when she pulled away from him then. He let her go, watched as she stared at her reflection a moment more, then turned that same anguished look on him.

"I did this for Miles," she told him, and there was something else in her voice he didn't recognize. "Because I never want to be the thing that holds him back. Not in anything." She waved a hand over her dress, her face twisting. "But I don't want to do *this* again."

"I don't know what you think that gown is doing to you. You're a beautiful woman. Why shouldn't you dress like one?"

"I'm an abandoned orphan from New Orleans," Shona said, grief showing on her face. Or perhaps it was closer to fury. "I come from nothing. I am nothing. I don't belong in a dress like this." She shook her head and laughed a little, though there was nothing like humor in the sound. "Yadira even tried to fit me with some kind of—"

"Jewels," Malak finished for her. "I know. I chose them myself."

"It's ridiculous." She threw the words at him like an accusation. As if it should have been a body blow that knocked him back a few feet, at the very least. "I don't know what you want. I know what I look like. I know exactly who I am."

"Then you had better tell me what you think that is. Because I'm afraid I am at a loss."

"You don't have to humiliate me," Shona whispered, and that, then, was the body blow. Malak was surprised he stood his ground. "I'm here, aren't I? You might think I scowl too much, but I haven't tried to escape, have I? I haven't tried to turn Miles against you. I haven't kept him from you. I haven't even argued with the way you've decided his time here should be spent. Even before you brought us here I agreed that you could see him. Isn't that enough? Why do you have to humble me as well?"

Her voice cracked and something inside Malak did the same. He took a step toward her and she moved away, but not with her usual grace. It was as if she stumbled, though she didn't trip. She simply moved, jerkily, over to the bench in front of the nearest fountain and sat there.

"There is nothing humble about you, little one," Malak said quietly, and maybe he was the one without his customary grace. "You are proud and you are strong and I pity any man who imagines he could humiliate you."

She made another sighing sound. "And yet you do it. You do it without even trying."

He closed the distance between them. She already looked like a queen. If he had ever imagined a queen, the images would have paled next to Shona. Her dark hair was full and curly around her head. The gorgeous deep green gown swept over her figure, as demure as it was alluring. Her skin gleamed, that rich brown that haunted him when he was awake and asleep, and she shone brighter than the sparkling water of the fountains or the intricate mosaics on the floor beneath their feet.

She was as perfect now as she had been in a gold dress and smile five years ago.

Even more so, perhaps, because she'd given him Miles.

"Shona," he started again, reaching over to take her chin in his hand. He tilted her pretty face to his.

"It's cruel," she whispered. Her eyes glittered with some kind of intense emotion he had no hope of naming, but he could feel it. Inside him. Around him. In his throat and his chest and his heavy sex. "You can dress me up. You can throw gowns on me and wrap ridiculous chains of impossible jewels around my neck. But it doesn't change anything. Don't you understand that? Nothing will ever change *me*."

"What do you think I want to change?"

She jerked her chin from his grip. "Everything."

It was the way she said that word. With too much heat and that brokenness besides.

"I don't want to change you, Shona."

"Of course you do." Her voice was thick but Malak didn't think the darkness in it was aimed at him. "I don't blame you. But I would rather the whole world see me for who I really am right from the start than this—this sad game of charades that no one will ever believe, anyway."

She made a hollow noise when he only stared at her.

"I don't believe that you can't see it. Weren't you the one who was just telling me how sad and narrow my life is? The truth is, you're right. I have nothing to give Miles now. I don't know how to raise a prince. I thought I was doing okay as a single mother making ends meet. Better than my own mother did, anyway. You can call me a queen. You can dress me up like one if you must." She pulled in a ragged breath, then let it out in a rush. "But you can't change the simple fact that I was thrown away like trash because I am trash. You can't dress that up no matter how hard you try."

Malak felt something deep inside him go still. Like rage turned to stone.

But he gazed at Shona with all the ease that had marked him in his playboy days. As if there was nothing heavy between them and never would be.

"I am the king of Khalia," he told her quietly. "Any woman I have ever slept with is, by definition, only of the highest caliber. Diamonds of the finest water, as they say. But the mother of my child? The mother of the next king of this glorious kingdom? It is impossible that this woman—this paragon who must be celebrated above all others as a matter of national pride and patriotic duty—can ever be or could ever have been anything remotely like trash."

"I think you're talking about Miles again."

"Quite apart from that," he said, with all the certainty of his station and the throne that had never felt more like his than it did today, "this is my country. You are whatever I say you are. And I must inform you that you are among the finest treasures of the kingdom, Shona. Because I say so."

Her lips curved, but her eyes were sad. "That doesn't make it true."

"Maybe this will convince you, then."

He did what he had been longing to do for what seemed like forever. He stepped closer to her, and swept her up from the bench, and into his arms at last.

And then finally—*finally*—Malak took her mouth with his.

CHAPTER NINE

IT WAS AS if Shona had been swept out to sea.

A wave of sensation crashed over her and dragged her off, tumbling her end over end and tossing her far away from anything like land. She knew she needed to swim in the few moments she had left before she began to drown.

But Shona didn't know how to swim. She wasn't sure she knew how to float. So instead, all she could do was cling to Malak as if he was a lifesaver when she knew very well he was the reason she was out there fighting to stay above water in the first place.

Not that any of that seemed to matter much when he kissed her.

He kissed her and he kissed her.

She didn't know how to keep track of all the feelings and sensations that swirled around her and inside her, so she poured herself into the kiss instead. She didn't know what she wanted—or she didn't know how to express it—so she stopped worrying about it and lost herself in the slick magic of his tongue against hers.

He'd called her out and then he'd called her treasure, and how could she be expected to handle that kind of whiplash?

She wound her arms around his neck. She stopped pretending that she didn't hunger for him with every part of the body that had already betrayed her so comprehensively out on that balcony.

His hands moved down the length of her back—though it hardly felt like *her* back at the moment, covered as it was in the finest fabric Shona had ever touched—and he made a low noise in the back of his throat when his palms moved over her bottom.

Then the world seemed to move in a dizzy little circle, and when it was done, he was sitting on that bench next to the fountain and she was on his lap, astride him, her back to his front.

He was that strong, she thought in a kind of dazed amazement. He could simply lift her and position her and do as he wished with her.

The notion made her shudder.

"I want you to watch," he told her, his voice low and gritty with that same need she could feel storming through her. Changing her. Altering the bones inside her skin. Making her imagine things she'd given up on so long ago she'd forgotten it was possible to want them in the first place. "I want you to tell me what you see."

They were reflected in so many different mirrors. Malak was beautiful, as big and broad as he was lean. He held her so easily, there on his lap with his strong arms wrapped around her waist, and try as she might, she didn't see anything resembling a treasure. She saw the same thing she'd seen in the reflection back in her rooms.

Seeing herself dressed up in a princess costume only pointed out how far away she was—and would always be—from ever being such a thing.

But she didn't feel the lurching, awful knot in the pit of her stomach anymore the way she had when she'd first caught sight of herself. And she knew it had everything to do with the way Malak's hands moved over her. His palms found her breasts and he lingered there, playing with pressure until she moaned and moved against him, wordlessly begging for more. She watched him track his way over her abdomen, then reach down farther, raking up the skirt of the long, emerald-green dress to expose her thighs.

And he didn't stop there. He pulled up the dress farther and farther, until she was sitting on his lap with only his trousers and her skimpy little panties separating them.

"I can feel your heat," he said against her ear, his voice as rough as it was warm against her skin.

Shona didn't want to look anymore. She wanted him, too, with a kind of desperate greed she was afraid to examine too closely. And those things fused together as she leaned back against the wall of his wide chest, angling herself so she could set her mouth to his again.

She lost herself in that kiss, again even as she felt his hands busy beneath them. He tugged at her panties until she felt the tugging give way and understood that he'd ripped them from her body.

It only made the way his tongue dueled with hers that much hotter. Better.

He broke the kiss, his hands at her hips. He lifted her up and laughed a little at the small noise of distress she made, then settled her down on his lap again—except this time, she could feel that extraordinary length of him between them.

Hard. Thick.

Hot.

Better by far than she remembered.

"Watch," Malak ordered her, his voice deliciously stern.

And Shona did.

His fingers dug into her hips as he lowered her, so slowly it was like an exquisite torture, onto the part of him that was hardest. The part of him she wanted most, as she melted in helpless longing. Her dress slid over her thighs again and hid what he was doing from view in those mirrors, so all she could see was Malak behind her, concentrating fiercely, and her own face.

Her own surrender was like a glare illuminating her.

Her eyes were wide and glazed and her neck felt like it could hardly bear the weight of her own head. Her lips parted as if she wasn't sure she could breathe and her hands had nothing to do but grip fistfuls of her dress.

It had been such a long time. It was almost as if this was new again: the way he stretched her, the way he filled her, the exquisite ache of his possession when he was finally fully settled inside her body.

Malak shifted then. He wrapped one arm around her and tilted her forward a little so that he moved even deeper within her.

And Shona felt it everywhere. Her toes. The tips of her ears.

"Go on then," he ordered her, his dark green gaze as fierce as emeralds, burning her into a crisp through the reflection of the glass in front of them. "Show me who you are."

And if there was the faintest shadow of some kind of argument inside her, she ignored it.

Shona began to move.

She tested the rotation of her hips. She rocked herself, forward and back, then in lazy circles.

She arched to dig her toes into the floor on either side of Malak's legs, and used that as leverage to pull herself up, then slide back down the entire delectable length of him. Once, then again. And again, until they both groaned.

He reached out and found her hands, then laced his fingers with hers as he crossed their arms over her abdomen, together.

And still she rocked against him. She practiced her strokes, reacquainting herself with something she hadn't realized she'd longed for, deep in the night, lost in dreams she'd pretended not to recall during the day.

Long and slow. Hard and fast.

His eyes blazed in the mirror. There was color high on those cheekbones of his, so sharp they made her feel like swooning even as he held her fast. He was as fierce as he was beautiful, like this place and the desert he ruled.

And she saw herself. The dizzy abandon on her face, that madness in her eyes, that she wasn't sure she'd ever seen before. She thought it might well be joy.

Shona hardly recognized herself.

And if it was a stranger, a little voice inside her whispered, *you would say she was beautiful. Because that woman in Malak's arms is beautiful.*

"I want…" she whispered, the words torn from her as if she had no control over them.

"Tell me," he growled, his mouth like a brand in the crook of her neck, and the strange thing was, she craved the burn of it. "Tell me what you want."

"I want you," she managed to say.

She felt his smile, wicked and dark, there against her heated skin—even as she saw it happen in the mirror. It was like having the same sensation twice. That much brighter. That much hotter. "You already have me. I'm deep inside you."

"Please," she moaned, as if it wasn't really begging. As if it was the most natural thing in the world to make these noises, to want these things she wanted, but only from him. "Please, Malak…"

"Tell me what you want," he said again, more fiercely this time. "Tell me what you need, Shona."

"I want…everything," she managed to say, dizzy from her own rocking. From the slick, endless slide up, then down, again and again, and him so intensely hard inside of her. "Please, Malak. *Please.*"

He freed one of his hands from her grip, then reached down between them, moving beneath the silk of her dress to find the place where they were joined. And his fingers were as wicked as they were clever.

Malak found the aching center of her need and pressed down.

"Your wish is my command." His voice was like another touch. "My queen."

And then he drove her straight over that edge.

Shona tumbled and soared, bliss chasing itself around and around, and Malak followed her over that same steep, glorious side of the world, calling out her name as he fell.

For a long time they stayed as they were, with Malak lodged deep inside her as if they'd been made to fit like that. Some part of her believed they had been. That every day they'd missed this connection, this perfect fit, had been a kind of crime.

Shona didn't want to move. She was limp against him, her head tilted back against his shoulder. And when she opened her eyes, she could see the two of them in the mirror still.

He was so big and he held her so easily. He made her feel fragile. Delicate. Precious…and she'd never felt like that in her life.

Shona waited to feel ashamed. To feel that kick of self-disgust. Or that same mocking voice that had chased her since the moment she'd stepped into this dress, telling her what a fool she was making of herself. Telling her how little she belonged here.

In this palace. With this man.

Telling her things she knew, down deep in her bones, were nothing more than the truth.

Because even before he'd become a king, she'd known that Malak wasn't for her. That the one night she'd had with him was more than she deserved.

But right now, she couldn't chase after those things the way she knew she probably should have, because all she could feel was Malak. He was still deep in her body, still broad and deep. He was made of steel and heat and he surrounded her. She could feel him when she breathed.

Everywhere.

As if he was a part of her.

"Look at you," Malak said quietly, and her eyes flew to his. Her heart kicked at her as she waited for that other shoe to hit her again, for him to say some of the things she'd already thought herself, to cast her aside the way she thought he should—but there was nothing but approval on his face. Nothing but that same lust and fire in his dark green eyes. "Look at us. How can you possibly doubt that you belong right here?"

Shona didn't know if he meant *here* in the palace, or *here* in his arms. And she didn't know why she didn't ask. Why she didn't scrape and claw at him with her bitter sarcasm the way she normally would have.

It was almost as if something inside of her had hushed. As if the volume of all that noise she carried around inside of her had been turned down.

And it didn't feel as if she'd lost something. It felt like a relief.

He didn't wait for her to answer. His eyes still blazed as he reached between them to disengage himself. And Shona couldn't help the small noise she made when he pulled out of her.

Malak stood, taking her with him as he rose. He set her on her feet before him, and then took a moment to tuck himself back into his trousers. Shona smoothed down her full skirt and thought it had been easier five years ago, in the dark of a hotel room. She'd drifted off to sleep and when she'd woken up again, he'd been gone.

No reflections in mirrors to contend with. No need to come up with any awkward conversation.

She searched for something, anything, to say. But Malak had other ideas. He swept her up into his arms again, then lifted her high against his chest, and that was better. Easier, anyway.

Shona had always imagined surrender differently. Drowning, maybe. But this was as easy as stepping into a warm bath.

And far, far better.

"Where are we going?" she asked as he began to move.

Malak didn't look down at her. He kept his eyes straight ahead as he walked, carrying her down the corridors of his palace.

"I'm not done with you yet," he said, and his voice was still all fire and greed. It twisted through her and lit her up all over again. "Not nearly."

And Shona thought on some level that she should fight that. Fight him. She should fight because that was what she did.

It was the only thing she'd ever known how to do. Her only skill. The only thing in this world she knew beyond a shadow of a doubt that she did well.

But she didn't have it in her. Not tonight. Not here

in a palace so far away from anything and everything she'd ever known.

So instead she rested her head against Malak's shoulder, let her eyes drift shut and let him carry her wherever he pleased.

When Shona woke in the morning she had no idea where she was.

It wasn't a new sensation.

Waking up without knowing where she was, in fact, was one of Shona's least favorite things in the world. She felt it in her stomach first, that sickening little lurch that she remembered all too well, because nothing felt familiar. She opened her eyes to find herself staring at something that didn't make any sense.

She could see bold red fabric shot through with gold, but she knew her bedroom here was done up in creams and blues.

The night before came back to her slowly. The way these things always did. It reminded her too much of waking up in strange foster houses as a child, never knowing where she was. But she didn't feel unsafe at all now.

And maybe that was what soothed her, as she took stock of her body, stretched out on a big, wide bed. She felt…protected, even as she tried to sort out what had happened. She felt a delicious tiredness all over, in her fingernails and her skin and the crook of her toes. Marvelously, beautifully used. As if every last inch of her had been—

Shona felt a hot flush move over her, as if from the inside out. Because she remembered, then, in a great, rolling wave of delirious heat. Every last inch, indeed.

Malak had been demanding—fierce and thorough.

She had lost track of how many times he had taken her, there in his dizzyingly vast suite of rooms, all of which were exactly as luxurious and over-the-top as she had expected, given what the rest of the palace looked like. Had there ever been room in her life for such foolishness?

Not that it was his bedroom that had captivated her, hour after hour.

She had learned how he tasted, everywhere. She had explored him as if he was hers. She'd had her mouth and her fingers on every inch of his beautiful body, reveled in that hot, smooth skin of his that looked like cinnamon and tasted all man. Hot and gloriously male.

He had taught her to take him deep in her mouth, either kneeling there at his feet or over him on the bed, propped up between his legs. He had made her scream, with his mouth between her legs again, and more outrageously, using nothing more than his fingers on one nipple and his teeth and a wicked bit of suction on the other.

The night had gone on and on, until it had all felt like liquid, pouring through her hands, impossible to hold, shimmering there whenever she turned her head too fast. And she hadn't given herself permission to brood. To worry. To do anything but enjoy what was happening there between them.

Again and again and again.

He had called for food at some point, and they'd eaten it together, there in the seating area somewhere beyond the foot of his bed. It was erected around a vast fireplace that looked as if ten men could stand inside it, though Malak had only laughed when Shona had said so. She had wrapped herself in one of the shockingly soft sheets from his bed, and they'd feasted on food that had ceased to seem strange to her, after all these weeks in Khalia. Dates and nuts and strong cheeses. Delicate pastries that melted in her mouth. Meats and casserole-type things that looked like lasagna but tasted far more complicated and airy.

And when they had both eaten their fill, Malak had crawled over her on the sofa where she'd been sitting and had told her he couldn't wait for dessert. Nor had he, as he'd pulled her hips up to his mouth again, until her cries had echoed off the walls.

She sat up carefully now, waiting to feel something pull, deep inside somewhere. She waited for the pain, because surely that was the price that had to be paid for a night like the one they'd shared.

She could hardly remember what had happened five years ago, or not this part of it, anyway. She remembered waking up in that hotel room, how hushed and uncertain she'd felt as she'd crept around, looking in all the rooms. There had been so many rooms, when all she knew about hotels were down-market motels, where a person was lucky to have a bed and a towel that didn't draw blood. But when she'd discovered he was not lurking in one of the other rooms of the suite, that he'd gone sometime before she'd woken up, she hadn't wanted to stay herself.

Luxury had made her uncomfortable. It seemed like some kind of…mockery, really. She had gathered herself as best she could, scrunching up her hair so that the curls looked springy again, and smoothed her dress back into place. Her heart had been pounding wildly in her chest when she'd walked out into the front hall that was still a part of the hotel suite, then taken the elevator that was right there down to the ground floor. She'd expected to be stopped at any moment, for one of the people who clearly belonged in a hotel as fancy as that one to question her; to ask her what on earth she thought she was doing in a nice place like that, when she was sure she had her humble beginnings written all over her.

But no one had said a word. And if they'd looked at her with any sort of judgment in their eyes, she hadn't looked closely enough at anyone she'd passed on her way out to have seen it. She'd escaped back into the bawdy French Quarter gratefully, feeling almost instantly at ease once she'd hit the streets. That was where she belonged. Not in some fancy hotel.

Here, now, she certainly didn't feel as if she should have been waking up alone in the king's bedchamber. It was worse than that hotel. It was…royal. Sunlight was streaming into the bedchamber from the grand archways that functioned as both windows and doors, leading out to another one of those polished marble balconies—this one wider and far grander.

Shona sat where she was, listening carefully. She held her breath, trying to hear any clues as to Malak's whereabouts. She'd learned how to be good at that kind of thing in too many foster homes to count. It was always better to have an idea of where everybody was under whatever roof she happened to find herself.

But she couldn't hear a thing. Fancy hotels and royal palaces were so *quiet.* She crept out of the bed, making sure her feet made no noise against the floor, covered as it was in fine rugs. She looked around for the gown that Malak had taken off her so slowly, so deliciously, the night before, but it was nowhere in sight. She frowned at that, because she was certain he had tossed it to the side right there on the floor. But it wasn't where she thought it should have been, over in the vast expanse between the side of his bed and the bathroom suite that could have housed an entire parish or two.

"You look confused," came Malak's voice from the doorway, rolling over her the way she began to realize it always would. As if he was connected to something inside of her and could tug on it at his leisure. "Not exactly a rousing endorsement of last night's festivities, I think."

"I was looking for my clothes."

"I cannot imagine why you think you need such things." He sounded amused. And something darker. Hotter. "When I am only going to remove them."

CHAPTER TEN

MALAK HELD OUT his hand and Shona didn't have it in her to refuse it.

Even though there was that noise inside her head, warning her of all the terrible ways this could end. All the other shoes that could fall and crush her, even in a palace like this—because they always, always did. Even though there was that hitch in her chest that she was terribly afraid was the heart she'd thought so well armored and so protected after all these years that nothing could ever come close to threatening it.

But on the other side of all of that was Malak, and that hand outstretched before her.

Unwavering and certain, as if he had no doubt whatsoever that she would take it.

And she couldn't seem to help herself. She reached out and slid her fingers into his.

He pulled her close and her body knew him now. She melted into him, and then, better by far, his mouth was on hers.

And it was still so good. His kiss was like light, heat and longing, despite the fact she would have told herself that she had nothing left in her. That she'd given all she had to give, long ago.

He led her out onto the marble balcony, bathed in the crisp, bright light of another desert morning. Then he led her off to the side, where a gleaming, rectangular pool sat on its own raised platform, part of the water beneath billowing canopies that provided some little bit of shade.

"I don't swim," she told him, but she didn't pull her hand from his. She didn't slow her stride. She didn't immediately launch herself into action—she just said it.

Almost as if you'll do anything the man asks you to do, a little voice inside her observed. But she pushed that aside, because there was a kind of fluttery sensation deep inside her and she didn't know how to name it. She didn't want to name it.

"You don't have to swim," Malak told her, his dark eyes glittering as if he knew. As if he knew everything that moved inside her, heat and disquiet and fluttering alike. "You need only float."

"I don't float."

Malak eyed her, standing there in all that desert sunlight, bright and clean and so unlike the thick Louisiana air she knew. He studied her face as if she was wearing some kind of mask when the funny thing was, she had never felt more exposed or raw.

"You come from a city that is below sea level. Of course you can float."

"I wouldn't know. Who had time for swimming lessons?" Shona laughed a little at that. Because the very notion was absurd. One of her foster parents setting aside time—and even more unlikely, money— to take Shona to unnecessary lessons? Impossible. The subject had never come up.

"Then this will be another first, little one," Malak told her. "We can only hope it will be even half as delightful—and instructive."

Shona felt hot at that, and she couldn't pretend it was the Khalian sun. Then she felt hotter still when Malak let go of her hand so he could strip himself of the loose, flowing white trousers which were all he had on—and which did nothing at all to direct attention away from the lean power of his sculpted body.

And the reality of what they were doing hit her, then. Standing outside, absolutely stark naked, together. In the brightness of the Khalian morning, where anyone could see them.

If anyone could see onto the king's private balcony, that was, which Shona doubted. But still.

Shona knew she should have been horrified. Embarrassed, at the very least. Her experiences of being naked or close to it around other people were limited to that hotel room with Malak all those years ago, the night she'd given birth to Miles and now.

She should have wanted to run and hide.

Especially since the man wanted her to get into a *pool*, of all things.

But she didn't run. She didn't even try to conceal herself. She watched as Malak climbed over the lip of the pool and then sank into the sparkling turquoise water until he was submerged up to his waist. He lifted up his hands and she took them, then let him help her down into the water's embrace.

He had taught her how to catch fire. How to lose herself in the slick, sweet beauty of one body deep inside another. He had taught her lust and longing, need and release.

All that and the fluttering that made her feel like a winged thing, bright and feathery, as if at any moment she might take flight.

But this bright morning, when she'd woken up alone only to find that she wasn't, after all, Malak taught her something else. He led her down into the water with him and held her in his strong grip, and he taught her how to float.

How to let the water hold her aloft, so that she really did feel like she was flying.

And he taught her something else, there where there was nothing but blue water below and blue sky above, and him in the center of it all, stern and sweet and his dark green gaze on her as if there had never been anything in all the world but the two of them together, just like this.

He taught her that the other shoe she'd feared

would fall was far more dangerous than any she could have imagined, before, when the only thing she had feared was the possibility of his reappearance.

It wasn't what he would do to her, out on a marble balcony with the desert light like a caress upon her face. It wasn't the water that coursed over her like the prayers she'd long since stopped saying. It wasn't all the things they'd done in that wide bed of his or in that atrium made of mirrors. It was much, much worse than those things and it was already done.

It was her poor little heart, that beat as if he was the only reason for it to exist in the first place, in this pool and in this palace and in the chaotic streets of the French Quarter, too.

It was the pride in his voice when he talked to or about their son.

And it was the way he took her, masterful and sure, right there in that gleaming turquoise pool so that she sobbed out her need and his name against his wide shoulder, as if she'd remembered how to pray, after all.

Shona had never fallen in love with anyone—had never wanted that kind of torment in her life when she'd never seen anything but too many examples of it going wrong—but maybe that was the point.

This wasn't falling, here with Malak. It was floating.

And she'd been doomed from the start.

* * *

After that night, Shona threw herself into all the things she'd ignored before, because if there was one thing she knew how to do, it was figure out how to make the best of things if there was no alternative.

Might as well fly if you're already falling, she told herself, and she tried to do just that.

Shona shocked her tutors by paying attention in her lessons. She actually wore the clothes that Yadira set out for her and tried to at least pretend to be the sort of woman who was comfortable in such fine fabrics and shockingly elaborate costumes. She didn't know the first thing about being a queen, but she knew how to pretend.

So that was what she did.

Because Shona also didn't know what to do with a heart that felt four sizes too big, and more painfully raw with every beat. She didn't know how to make sense of the things she felt, or the man who made her feel them. So she did what she could instead.

She told herself it was for Miles.

"You're so pretty, Mama," he told her one evening as they made their way to their usual dinner in the king's private rooms.

"Thank you, baby," she said, smiling down at him, aware that there were only so many evenings left that he would happily hold her hand as they walked. And only so many days left when she could snuggle his whole body with hers before he grew too big—

and before he stopped allowing her to hold him that way at all.

"You're much prettier here than you were before," he told her with all that stout, four-year-old certainty. "It's much better."

Shona wanted to correct him, but she couldn't, because much as it shamed her to think such a thing, he was probably right.

Miles had bloomed here. He was happier than he'd ever been. He laughed more. He was joyful and playful and *bright*. She couldn't let herself dwell on it too closely or she was afraid she might lapse into some kind of retroactive depression…because the truth was, she'd thought they were fine in New Orleans. She'd thought Miles was fine. She'd thought they were absolutely doing their best—and they'd certainly been doing better than she ever had when she'd been his age.

Maybe all of that was true. But maybe her measure of these things was off. And more than a little sad. Because there was no getting past the fact that Miles was far better off here. He slept well, ate well and never acted out in the ways he had back home. If Shona was honest with herself, she had always felt so guilty she couldn't spend the kind of time with him she had wanted to because she'd had to work so hard to pay their bills.

Here, if she wanted, she could spend whole days exploring the extensive palace gardens with her son if that took his fancy. They could spend hours watching movies in the middle of a Wednesday morning if they chose. She could do whatever she wanted with him. They could play, or if he caught a cold, he could snuggle up at her side and sleep it away. She never had to worry about picking up an extra shift. Or how she was going to make rent if she called in sick—or whether she dared do such a thing at all, no matter how sick Miles was, because she'd lose her job if she tried.

It shocked her how much happier Miles was here, without the weight of all that forever pressing down on them.

But she was equally shocked by how much happier *she* was.

For all of those reasons and more.

It was as if she'd had no idea how heavy all that weight was until she'd put it down. And now she couldn't understand how she'd carried any of it in the first place.

"You look like a queen should," Miles told her another morning when she came out of her dressing room to find that he was still sitting there, cross-legged on her bed, instead of off with his nannies the way he normally was after breakfast.

She still didn't like that word. *Queen.* She still had to fight to pretend she thought it could apply to her. It still ate at her in ways she didn't like, and it shocked her how deep that went. How dark it made her feel to look at herself dressed up like a stranger.

When all she wanted was to belong. In her own reflection. In these absurd clothes she wore now. In this fairy-tale palace she'd never dared let herself dream about.

Somewhere, the foster kid inside of her whispered. *I just want to belong* somewhere.

She wanted to growl something dismissive at Miles to make sure he never said anything like that again, but she didn't. Because there was something about seeing pure love and pride on her baby's face that kept her usual disparaging remarks inside her own mouth.

"Do you think?" she asked him.

Miles nodded enthusiastically. "You're queen and Papa is king. And I'm the prince."

"You're the crown prince," she said, agreeing with him.

"And you have to marry Papa," Miles continued, matter-of-factly. "Or it won't work."

"What won't work?" She had to fight to keep her emotions out of her voice. After all, Miles was only four. He didn't necessarily know what he was saying. For all she knew he was just parroting one of his nannies.

"The king and the queen have to be married, Mama," Miles replied, looking at her as if she was crazy. "Everybody knows that."

"Sometimes mamas and papas don't get married," she told him, ignoring the instant cluck of disapproval from Yadira, who was still bustling around inside the dressing room and could hear every word. Shona still wasn't used to that—to never being truly alone. But this wasn't the time to worry about that. "That's perfectly okay, you know. Marriage isn't for everyone."

"Maybe for mamas and papas who aren't kings and queens," Miles said, rolling his eyes. "But you're a queen, Mama."

As if it was something that went without saying. And so obvious that only a fool could possibly think otherwise.

And Shona didn't know why, but there was something about Miles's easy acceptance of her as a queen that…eased its way inside her.

Or maybe, if she was honest, it had more to do with Miles's father. The demanding, focused and inventive Malak, who never stopped playing games with Shona—especially because now, they both won.

Sometimes he would insist that she stand through part of dinner, so he could make good on his threat and eat her alive as his dessert. He took her to his bed every night, and Shona kept waiting for the things they did there to grow old. Familiar.

Because all she'd known of sex and men was that one night long ago. Until another night five years later.

But it turned out that nights with Malak grew better the more of them there were. Deeper. Darker.

More and more magical the more time she had to learn him.

It turned out that Shona was a much better student than she'd ever imagined, back when she'd struggled to make it through this or that high school. Always the new girl. Always temporary. Always behind or ahead of the rest of the class. Always out of sync.

But not here.

She made progress with her Arabic. She learned how to walk like a queen. How to sit like a queen. How to handle herself when faced with the sorts of world leaders who would inevitably find their way to Malak's side and who would hope to weasel their way closer to him through her.

All day she studied how best to become a queen while at night she learned more and more ways to come alive beneath the hands of the only man who had ever touched her. The only man she wanted to touch.

As far as she was concerned, Malak was the only man in the world. And he made her feel as if she was the only woman he'd ever laid eyes on.

Shona wasn't sure she had ever felt so alive in her life.

So alive. And so in love with him, despite herself. When she'd always thought she was immune to such things—that love was a failing, not a joy. It was as if every hour was electric now. As if everything was new, even if she'd done it time and time again.

And that was why, the next time Malak called her his queen, she nodded.

She was stretched over him in his bed, her heart still thundering inside her chest. And better yet, she could feel his beating hard, too.

She had ridden him until they both tipped over into bliss, and then she'd collapsed against him the way she always did. His hands still held her bottom, his thumbs moving in rhythmic little circles. This way, then that.

But he went very still when she nodded, moving her head against his chest.

"I beg your pardon? Are you trying to tell me something?"

Because this was Malak. He would not accept a quiet surrender when a loud one would do.

Shona pushed herself up into a sitting position again, sucking in a breath when she felt him, still deep inside her. She felt boneless and wrung out, but all he needed to do was shift his hips and that changed in an instant. She could feel that glorious fire turn over deep inside her, as if she had an ignition switch that only he knew. She could feel the flames begin to lick against her. Everywhere they touched.

The way they always did.

She braced her hands against his chest and gazed

down at him, unable, still, to make sense of all of this. Because it felt too good. It felt too…right. Malak hardened again deep inside of her as if he, too, could never get enough. His beautiful body, hers to touch like this.

To claim, something whispered inside of her.

As if he was hers.

She, who had never had anything.

"I will be your queen, Malak," she told him.

She had meant to sound funny. Or wry, anyway. Light and airy and offhand.

But there in the dark of his bedroom it sounded a great deal more like a solemn vow.

And she could see the way his dark eyes gleamed. "Will you indeed."

"I will," she said again.

And she moved her hips then, smiling when he responded instantly and surged against her. It was a flame that would never, ever go out, because it lived between them. It was theirs.

She let her smile turned wicked. "For Miles, of course."

"Of course," Malak replied, his voice little more than a growl. "I commend your maternal instinct."

And then Shona was laughing because Malak flipped them over in the bed, coming over her to drive himself deeper inside of her, taking complete control.

And she surrendered.

Her heart was too full. She wanted too much. She had never imagined that she could risk herself this way—

But how could that matter? He was a king. He called her his queen. And better still, her son looked at them both as if they had never been anything but.

Mostly, she thought as Malak surged inside of her, it was him.

It was Malak.

And maybe that was why, when he drove her over the side of the world this time, she tipped her head back and cried out the one thing she had never said to another man. Or any other person alive, besides her son.

"I love you, Malak," she sobbed, because she had to say it out loud or burst with the force of it. *I love you.*

CHAPTER ELEVEN

THE FIRST TIME Shona told him she loved him, Malak did her the great courtesy of ignoring the outburst.

He assumed it was the heat of the moment. The fact they were in bed had obviously confused her and made her lose all sense and reason. After all, he reminded himself, this was all very new to her. He chose to take it as a compliment, nothing more.

Because Malak told himself she could not possibly realize what it was she had said. Or if she did, she would likely be so embarrassed by blurting out something like that, something that was mad and impetuous and plainly absurd, that she would never let that sort of thing fall from her lips again.

But the strangest thing happened in the days that followed: Shona didn't stop. She wasn't embarrassed at all, or if she was, she certainly didn't show it in any way Malak could understand.

On the contrary, it seemed that once Shona had accepted her role as his queen and the more she readied herself to take her place at his side, the more… reckless she grew.

There was no other word for it.

The word *love* fell from her lips with alarming regularity. And every time she said that damn word—or sobbed it, or moaned it, or whispered it as she slid off into sleep—it was as if she'd picked up a hammer and wielded it directly against his flesh.

Again and again and again, leaving nothing but wounds and bruises behind.

Still, Malak forced himself to remain quiet. To pretend none of that was happening. He kept hoping that if he continued to ignore it, if he acted as if she'd said nothing at all, Shona would stop letting that poisoned word escape her lips.

After all, there was a wedding to plan, one that befit Malak's new station and allowed his people to properly celebrate all the changes in the kingdom. There were delicate negotiations to pick his way through, inside his family and out. He had to invite his half brother, Adir, who ruled a desert tribe—and more importantly, had helped himself to Zufar's original betrothed after an unfortunate confrontation at the palace. He had to invite his brother, Zufar, of course, who had abdicated the Khalian throne to rule with his new bride in remote Rumadah. And he had to invite his sister, Galila, and her husband, King Karim of Zyria, who happened to be the son of the man who had been Malak's mother's lover all those years ago. The royal diplomacy would have been headache enough. The seething family drama beneath all that diplomacy, though significantly calmer of late, made it all that much more of a minefield.

Because they were all coming, not only to celebrate Malak's wedding, but to show that the royal family of Khalia, though rocked by all that had happened since Queen Namani had died, stood proud and solid, together.

Malak told himself it was that alone that ate at him, dripping like acid into his heart. His gut. He told himself it was nothing but the same old family nonsense that had nearly destroyed them all already, a hundred times over. All those old secrets and new bonds that had caused so much upheaval, and had ended with Malak on the Khalian throne.

But it wasn't his family who haunted him. It wasn't their voices he heard in his head when he was trying to concentrate on his responsibilities.

It was Shona. It was always Shona. It was the way she said "I love you," over and over, and never seemed the least bit concerned that he failed to respond. Or even to acknowledge that she'd spoken at all.

And yet she slept so easily, sprawled over him or cuddled beside him in his bed. She slept the deep and restorative sleep of the righteous while Malak was the one left wide-awake and staring into nothing, those damn words going round and round inside of him.

Leaving marks wherever they touched.

One day, not long after Shona had started this campaign of hers to ruin what they had between them and drive him fully mad, Malak found himself up in the old family wing of the palace. He had been on his way to a stuffy meeting with his financial advisors and had taken a wrong turn. Then kept right on going.

His mother was gone now. His brother and sister had married and moved away. Malak himself had moved from the family wing to take his place in the monarch's traditional suite. Now the only inhabitant of these rooms Malak knew so well was his father.

His poor, lonely, broken father, whom Malak had always seen as a victim of love. Even when Tariq had still been king and Namani had still been alive and they'd both continued to put a happy face on their wretched marriage.

Today Malak found the old man in what had once been a playroom but was now the abdicated king's personal library. And as he stood in the doorway, Malak remembered finding his father exactly like this, across all the years of his childhood. When he wasn't off ruling the kingdom, Tariq had found an armchair in the family wing and had sat as he did now, a book open in his lap but his gaze fixed somewhere on the other side of the nearest window.

As a child, Malak had imagined his father had been consumed with weighty ruminations regarding the kingdom, the future, his role as king. He'd imagined his father had stared out and seen his own consequence, his own power—both of which Malak had found fascinating as none of that had ever been meant to be his.

He knew now that it was far more likely that the old man had been brooding over the unfaithful wife who had never loved him.

All that power and consequence was Malak's after all, for his sins. And it didn't escape him that all *he* seemed to think about was the woman he was about to marry who couldn't stop telling him she loved him, when he knew exactly where that led.

Here, he thought darkly. *It leads right here.*

To a lonely old man in a chair, hidden away in a room filled with memories, ghosts and grief.

Malak stayed where he was in the doorway rather than walking in, as too many competing emotions were roaring through him at once. None he particularly liked. He loved his father. There could be no argument on that score, but it was also true that when he looked at the old man—particularly locked away up here, where nothing could distract him from his endless focus on Namani—he felt a kind of sorrow that knew no name.

A sort of grief, perhaps, for what might have been. Had his father been a different man. Had his mother been a woman worthy of the kind of devotion the old king had lavished upon her no matter the cost to him, his kingdom or their children. Had either one of his parents thought less about themselves and the tangle of their personal lives and a little bit more about the children they should have been attempting to raise.

Malak had always talked himself out of that kind of harsh judgment in the past. Yes, his parents had ignored their children, but it was not as if they had been run-of-the-mill, suburban parents somewhere. They had been King Tariq and Queen Namani of Khalia. They could hardly have been expected to spend the kind of time with their offspring that others with fewer responsibilities did.

They had always had to think of Khalia first.

He had long assured himself that he was being unfair to imagine he should hold his parents to any kind of selfish, imaginary standard, simply because he might have liked some more attention. All the kingdoms of the world were littered with the ignored offspring of royal parents and yet, somehow, the kingdoms carried on.

Besides, Malak had always flourished in all that space he'd been given, with no one to pay the slightest attention to anything he did.

Except now Malak had Miles. He doubted very much that he was any less busy than his father had been, especially as his father had not inherited a throne in the midst of such turmoil with successive abdications. And still, Malak somehow managed to spend time every day with his son. His child, who had spent four years of his young life apart from his father already—something Malak had no intention of repeating as long as he drew breath.

It turned out he was less sympathetic to Tariq than he had been when he'd been single and carefree and hadn't known what it was like to feel such a fierce love inside of him, to feel the kind of madness that told him he would do anything at all for his own child—except pretend Miles didn't exist.

"Will you enter the room? Or stand there in the doorway forever?" his father asked mildly, his gaze still directed out the window where, Malak knew, the desert rolled and beckoned.

There was a time when it would have filled Malak with awe that his father knew he had approached when he'd made no sound. He had believed that his father was some sort of god who could see through walls. Clay feet were far less appealing than god-like powers and he thought, all things considered, he would have preferred the magic.

Especially when he felt so devoid of it himself.

But Malak only smiled and moved farther into the room. "I did not wish to disturb your reading."

He wondered why he bothered to pretend at all. Why he bothered to produce a smile, simply because he was Malak and a carefree, easy smile was what he was known for. And at the end of the day, it appeared that no matter if he took the throne or not, he still behaved the fool when given the opportunity. It was some kind of knee-jerk reaction when speaking to members of his family, maybe. All of whom had pledged their support to him—but none of whom had ever thought he'd make any kind of *good* king, or any kind of king at all, before Zufar's abdication.

Malak was the only *available* king. He never forgot that.

But when he looked at his father, who had been promised to the throne and to Khalia since the moment of his birth, he couldn't help but think that might be for the best. Because Malak had lived the gift of his birth as the spare.

He thought perhaps he was the only clear-eyed king that Khalia had had in years.

Maybe that was why he knew exactly where the last two kings had gone wrong.

"My aides have told me you are to be married, after all." His father closed the book on his lap and finally aimed that gaze of his at Malak. "There appeared to be some doubt, but I'm told it has now been settled."

How funny it was, Malak thought, that he was now the king and his father nothing but an old man with family connections, and yet when Tariq looked at him in that particular manner Malak still felt like a rowdy teenager called to account for his behavior. Perhaps that never faded, no matter who called himself king.

Perhaps that had more to do with the fact this man was still his father.

Or the fact that he'd shown interest in Malak so rarely that it had always seemed like a grand occasion when he did.

"Marriage was always inevitable in this case," Malak said, with perhaps a shade too much intensity. Then he shrugged it off. "But it is a major life change for Shona, of course. She has never been around royalty before. It's not surprising she needed some time to get used to the idea."

Maybe he'd given her too much time. Maybe that was the trouble. Maybe that was why she kept saying…that little piece of insanity. That sheer impossibility.

The thing that was precisely what he'd vowed would never taint his rule.

"She seems like a practical girl," his father was saying. "Exactly what you need, I imagine."

Malak found his hand on his chest, rubbing at his own heart as if the beat of it hurt him. He forced it back to his side. And opted not to examine why it was everything in him objected to hearing his father call Shona *practical*.

When she was so much more than that. When she was the only creature he'd ever beheld who could dim the desert sun when she smiled.

And more, why his father imagined Malak was the one who required a practical mate. When Malak was not the one who had given up a kingdom for the love of a woman who could barely contain her disdain for him in return.

But that was not something he could say to his father.

"You had a queen," he said instead, before he knew he meant to bring up such a fraught topic at all. But he managed to keep himself from making any accusations. "Have you any advice?"

"On the care and feeding of the average Khalian queen?" His father laughed, and it was only when the sound echoed back from the books lining the walls that it occurred to him that it had been a long while since he'd heard his father make that sound. Or do anything even remotely joyful. Once again, he found that complicated sadness moving in him. Grief, he thought, for a man who had never existed. And would never exist. "I don't think you need me to give you a dissertation about my failures in that arena. They are legion. And entirely public, to my shame."

Maybe this was why Malak had come here today, when he was meant to be neck-deep in tedious discussions elsewhere. To finally have this exact conversation he had never dared to begin with his father. To clear this last bit of air before Malak took the final step that would make him just like the old man.

In more ways than one, he thought darkly, Shona's voice in his head. Again.

Still.

"You loved her," he said, and fought to make that sound like something other than an indictment.

His father's gaze met his. And held. "I did. I still do."

"How?" Malak shook his head. "When you knew…?"

He couldn't say it. He couldn't talk euphemistically about *indiscretions* when both he and his father knew exactly what Namani had done. Moreover, Malak found that despite the fact he'd never understood his mother, nor wanted to spend any time with a woman who clearly hated him—because he was no substitute for Adir, the child she'd given away before she'd fallen pregnant with Malak—he didn't quite have it in him to tear her apart, either.

"Love does not change when it is tested," his father said slowly, as if it hurt him to speak of it. Or as if he had spent a long time coming to that conclusion. "If anything, it deepens. Which is not to say it does not become…more complicated."

"But surely there are some betrayals that make it impossible to keep loving another."

Or there ought to have been, surely.

"I'm the last person on earth who should offer marriage advice, Malak," his father said after a moment. "But I will tell you this. Life is filled with regrets, and I think any king's rule must be as well. It is the nature of the throne. But while you may regret political decisions, at length, you will never regret love. No matter what happens."

They moved to other topics, such as the wedding that would so soon take over the whole of the kingdom. And the goodwill the wedding would usher into the kingdom. But when Malak left his father to his reading again, all he could think about was what the old man had said about love.

He didn't understand why he couldn't get away from *love*, of all things, when he'd lived his whole life without it. Happily.

It was the love of a woman that had ruined his father. It had turned a decent ruler into a man obsessed with his careless, selfish wife above the good of his people, and certainly above the welfare of his own children. It was the love of a man not her husband that had given Malak's mother a child she'd had to give away, making it impossible for her to love the children she'd kept. It was the love of a woman that had led his brother to abdicate the throne, too, throwing the kingdom into more chaos it didn't deserve.

It was love that had stuck Khalia with Malak when the people deserved a more thoughtful king and a far better man. A man with the dignity the throne deserved instead of a sybaritic playboy who had been content to while away his days between any willing pair of thighs he could find.

Malak wanted nothing to do with *love*, thank you.

He wanted to rule his people with a cool head and a steady hand. He wanted to make certain that emotion could never again destroy the kingdom.

Much less another Khalian king.

He found himself walking faster and faster as he moved through the palace, hardly seeing the servants and aides who leaped out of his path. He didn't stop until he'd made it to Shona's rooms. He pushed through the doors and ignored how harsh his own breathing was. Particularly when he couldn't find her.

Malak kept going, making his way into the adjoining suite that belonged to Miles. Shona was there, playing some kind of game with Miles out on their balcony, surrounded by enough toy trucks to take over the kingdom.

He stopped there in the open balcony doors, watching them, his heart beating too hard. Too fast.

His father might not regret what he'd done for love, but Malak did. He lived his father's choices every day. His father's, his mother's and his brother's.

Love had consequences. Love was ruinous. How could the old man not see that, after all that had happened?

And how could Malak see anything else?

Shona would be his queen. Both of them could love Miles as the child deserved, and would. He knew they already did.

But he also knew, deep down inside of him, that

he had to put a stop to this nonsense about Shona loving him before he was tempted to imagine he could reciprocate it.

Because he knew exactly where that ended up. It was why he'd avoided such emotional entanglements the whole of his adult life.

He wanted what they already had. Sex. Laughter. Miles and whatever babies might come in the future. A partnership far better than the one he'd seen his parents attempt all those sad, tense years.

But there was no need to muddy it up with *love*. He had a kingdom to rule, and that meant he needed stability. Not the constant ebb and flow of love and all the wreckage that wrought.

He was so busy scowling that he didn't notice Shona had gotten to her feet and crossed the wide balcony to him until she was right there in front of him.

She was still the prettiest thing he'd ever seen. She glowed, especially when she frowned at him with *concern* all over her face. She made his chest hurt and God help him, but he was tired of *hurting*.

He understood that it was too late. That there was a reason everything hurt. That he was as much a fool as his brother and father before him.

But unlike them, he didn't have to act on the things he felt. He didn't need to call the feelings inside of him love. He didn't have to ruin himself and his kingdom over the ache in his chest.

He bloody well wouldn't.

"Is something wrong?" Shona asked.

"Nothing is the matter," he told her gruffly. He tilted his head in a silent command that she should follow him inside, leaving Miles in the care of his nannies, and was gratified when, for once, she followed without argument. "The wedding is being planned as we speak. It will be a vast celebration, appropriate for the king of these lands and the woman he claims as his."

"That sounds medieval."

"It sounds appropriate," he responded, correcting her. "But Shona…" He stopped when they had moved deeper into the rooms, out of earshot of the balcony. He hardly spared a glance for the sitting room he found himself in, all embroidered pillows and low tables, and he despaired of himself when all he could seem to think about was getting her naked and putting all those pillows to use. "You must never speak of loving me again. I find it offensive in the extreme."

She blinked. Then laughed, as if he'd started a comedy routine. "What? You find it *offensive*?"

"That is an order." He stepped back when she would have reached out and touched him and told himself he didn't care that she looked crestfallen. That it was better that way. "It was the fashion many years ago to lock up the queen in a far-off garrison, the better to ensure that she could never be used against the kingdom. Do not force me to take this step. Because I will if I have to."

"You want to…lock me up?" she asked, and she sounded…off. Weak, almost, as if he'd punched her in the stomach. He hated himself as if he really had. "In a garrison? Is that another way of saying *jail*?" She shook her head. "I don't understand what you're talking about, Malak."

"It is entirely up to you," he told her, stiff and dark. "I am giving you the power to decide what happens next and you should take that as the act of benevolence it is. You will become my queen either way, but I will not have this talk of love. It has no place here."

But all he could hear was her voice, sweet and soft in the night. The way she smiled when she tipped back her head and threw herself over into all that fire, all that heat, as if his hands, his mouth and his body were a kind of glory.

The way she said those terrible words he couldn't allow.

"Why not?" she asked now, and her voice sounded stronger. When she met Malak's gaze, he found he couldn't read her expression at all. It made his skin seem to tighten over his bones. "Is this your way of telling me I've forgotten my place?"

"Your place is at my side," he told her, forcing himself to sound cold. Forbidding. "I have told you this. But that doesn't mean we need to pretend that

what's between us is some kind of romantic fairy
tale. It's not. It never was, was it?" And because she
only stared at him as if he was speaking in tongues,
he let the curve of his lips edge into cruelty. "I think
you'll find that fairy tales seldom begin drunkenly,
in bars, between strangers."

He watched her take a deep breath and took no
pleasure at all in the fact he'd clearly hurt her. But
he didn't relent.

"Let me make sure I'm understanding you,"
Shona said after a long moment and with too much
vulnerability on her face. "I'm good enough to pa-
rade around in fancy clothes. I'm definitely good
enough to roll around naked in your bed. But if I
have any kind of feelings about those things and
worse, say them out loud, I'm out of line. Is that it?"

Something in him cracked at that, as if the faint
tremble in her lips was a fissure deep inside of him.

"Do not make me regret that I took the pleasant
path with you," he growled at her. "That I opted to
use honey rather than vinegar when I could so easily have simply taken what I wanted. Because you
wanted it, too."

"I don't know why you're acting like a monster
when you're not one."

But that was the problem. He felt like a monster
and she was to blame for that. She tempted him to
become the worst he was capable of. She was too
much temptation. She would ruin him.

She already had.

"You have no idea who I am or what I'm capable of," he told her. "Do not make me show you."

But Shona wasn't like any other woman he'd ever known. She didn't crumble. She didn't weep in awe or gratitude.

She only eyed him, then tilted that chin up as if she was fully prepared to fight him.

He understood that his ruin was complete.

"Show me," she dared him. "Tell me that you don't want me. Tell me to my face when you and I both know better."

And Malak didn't even hesitate. Because he knew that if he did, he would never do this. And then what would become of him? Of his kingdom?

"I wanted Miles," he told her, a deliberate and vicious blow, and the only wonder was that she didn't fall to her knees. "I never wanted you, Shona. Why would I? You're nothing to me but a means to an end."

And then he turned on his heel and left her there, that stunned look in her brown eyes and her mouth open in shock, before he proved exactly how weak he was—how very much his father's son he was, despite everything—and took it all back.

CHAPTER TWELVE

FOR A LONG time after Malak left, Shona simply... stood there.

She felt empty, somehow. As if he had done more than simply *say* those things to her. It was as if he'd dug into her with his fingers and scraped out her insides, leaving her hollow. Almost unbearably raw.

And altered straight through.

She didn't know how much time passed, but eventually she realized what she was doing. Standing stock-still in one of the entirely too many sitting rooms in this palace. In this suite of rooms, for that matter.

What four-year-old required a selection of seating areas?

But her attempt to manufacture some irritation on that score faded almost immediately, as if it had never been.

Because this particular sitting room was fitted with billowing tapestries and the kind of pillows people here used as chairs scattered all over every surface. There were golds and silvers, mosaics on the floor and some parts of the walls, and thick, patterned rugs thrown here and there.

But worst of all, there was a mirror that took up the whole of the far wall. The fact that it, too, was made of gold and precious stones only made it worse.

Shona stared at herself. She could see her chest rise and fall too quickly. She could see the faint sheen on her skin that broadcast exactly how flustered she was, in case she might have missed that on her own.

Though *flustered* was a weak way to describe how she felt.

It hardly touched on the swirling darkness that threatened to take her over. That threatened to drop her where she stood, and leave her there for Yadira to find, crumpled on the floor like the trash she'd always been.

Shona didn't let herself fall. She refused to crumple. She frowned at her reflection instead.

She had tried to get used to this new version of herself. She had *tried*. She had done her best to attempt to see herself through Miles's eyes instead of her own. She had tried to let the way Malak touched her, tasted her and made her feel far more beautiful than any woman ought to, be her guide.

But the words she most feared whirled around and around in her head and all she could see when she looked in that mirror was her own folly.

She was no princess. This was no fairy tale.

And she had been insane to imagine that her story could ever end differently.

How had she ever managed to imagine otherwise for even a moment?

She knew that woman in the mirror. Shona knew what mattered wasn't the shape of her face or the way she filled out yet another one of the gowns she found laid out for her each day. It didn't matter that this morning, when she'd dressed after another long night with Malak, she had actually smiled at this very same image. She'd found something hopeful in it. In *her*. There had been a light in her own eyes that she'd never seen before. She'd felt pretty, and more than that, something perilously close to happy.

She should have known better.

Shona had never yet made it through anything resembling a good moment without that other shoe crushing her flat. How could she possibly have imagined that this time it would be different?

"It's never different," she whispered to herself, as fiercely as she could when she felt as if she was nothing but jagged pieces of a broken thing. "It's never, ever different."

She heard Miles call for her from one of the other rooms, and pulled herself together. Painfully. She smoothed her hands over her dress, though her palms were damp. She straightened. She smoothed out her expression and forced herself to smile.

She knew better than to give in to the feelings that

slapped at her and beat her over the head then. Just as she should have known better than to give in to that other feeling that she'd foolishly given voice to over and over again.

The truth was, she'd known better as she was doing it. She'd known. But she'd gone ahead and done it, anyway.

She had no one to blame but herself for that sick feeling deep in her belly now.

"Enjoy," she muttered at herself as she left that awful sitting room and its terrible mirror and went to find her little boy.

Shona spent the rest of the afternoon with Miles, forcing herself to act calm and normal and *fine*, but all the while her head spun around and around. And Malak's words echoed inside of her as if he'd tattooed them on her rib cage.

Maybe if he had, it would have hurt her less.

Would Malak really send her off to some stronghold out there in the desert somewhere? Had she truly done this to herself? All by herself? Had she made all of this up—all the things she'd been so certain were building there between them?

But Shona couldn't answer any of her own questions. And the more they spun around inside of her, the more ill they made her feel.

When Yadira came to tell her, with her usual polite smile that Shona sometimes wanted to peel off her face by any means necessary, that the king would be dining elsewhere that evening, Shona wasn't surprised.

It felt like a kick to the ribs when she was already down, but she wasn't *surprised*.

She and Miles ate together instead, sitting on pillows low to the ground because Miles still thought that was almost too much fun to bear. When Miles asked where his papa was, she told him that his father was a very busy man who might often have to spend time away from them to do the things he needed to do as a mighty king. And she wondered if this would be her life now. If she would make up story after story to explain Malak's absence, or if she would be the one who was exiled. And if she was locked away somewhere, what stories would Malak tell Miles to explain her absence away?

A lump stuck in her throat.

She shooed away the nannies and put Miles to bed herself as if they were in their own, rattly house in New Orleans instead of a vast suite tailor-made for the crown prince. She tucked him into his big, wide bed that he liked to pretend was a spaceship and she read him story after story, and then she stayed with him as his breath became deep and even.

She had pulled the sumptuous curtains closed so Miles's room was dark, with only the faint gleam of the night-lights the nannies had placed at intervals casting happy little glowing circles in the corners of the big room.

Shona finally understood that her son was a prince. She understood, whether she liked it or not, that this was the reality they lived in now and there was no getting away from it. But there was more than a little part of her that rebelled at the notion that her sweet little Miles, so happy and so bright, might one day turn into another version of his father. Or his grandfather.

Malak, who touched her like she was made of fire then told her coldly he had never wanted her at all. Or the old king, whom Shona had only seen in passing, shuffling through the palace halls with a thousand-yard stare and nothing but whispers in his wake. She didn't want to see Miles become either one of them.

She didn't want her son growing up like all the broken men whose homes she'd lived in as a child. She'd seen ruin in all its forms. Substance abuse. Pure cruelty, simply because they could. Because no one cared. She'd seen poverty and selfishness and, worst of all, good intentions gone horribly wrong.

She didn't want any of that for Miles. She wanted him whole. Happy.

As bright as he was now. As he was meant to be forever.

Why don't you want that for yourself? asked a tiny little voice deep inside of her.

At first she tried to ignore it. She concentrated on the sweetness of the moment. Just her and Miles, curled up on a bed together, the way it always had been before. Her and Miles against the world.

But that little voice was insistent.

And the more it poked at her, whispering questions she didn't know how to answer, the more Shona found herself turning all of this over and over inside of her. As if her whole life was some kind of shivering thing that had taken her over tonight, and she couldn't control it at all.

Why did she accept it when someone made her feel like trash, even if that someone was the only man she'd ever loved? Why did she agree with his assessment when some part of her knew—she *knew*—that he'd been deliberately trying to hurt her? She would take great pleasure in ripping apart anyone who dared do that kind of thing to her child—so why couldn't she stand up for *herself*?

"You're not a whiner," she whispered at herself, there in the dark, while Miles slept beside her. "You're a fighter."

If she could fight and survive in New Orleans all these years—from foster care to the life she'd carved out for herself with absolutely no help from anyone—she should certainly be able to do the same here, where she was more pampered than she'd ever imagined any person could be.

But she couldn't help thinking that she'd spent her whole life fighting for the wrong things.

That notion tasted sour in her own mouth, but that didn't make it any less true.

She'd fought for some kind of safety, always. She'd fought to keep herself protected—by any means necessary. She'd fought to keep her child safe, too. To keep them both under a roof. To keep predators away from the both of them, one way or another. She'd fought and she'd fought, even if that fight had often meant cutting off her nose to spite her face.

And the notion that Miles might ever have to do any of that—for any reason—made her feel even more broken than she had in that sitting room earlier.

She pulled in a breath and tried to steady herself, but that feeling didn't go away. If anything, as she was lying there with her hand on Miles's back, feeling that little-boy heat of his fill her palm, it got worse.

Shona didn't want that kind of life—*her life*—for Miles. She would die before she would let him live the way she had. Always desperate. Always suspicious. Always waiting to get knocked down again. She would *die*.

So why was it she so easily accepted it for herself? As if it was no more than her due?

Shona didn't realize she meant to move. It seemed like some kind of dream. She had a simple enough thought about what she ought to accept for herself— and then the world changed. Or she did, anyway.

She was on her feet before she knew it. Then she

was in the halls, wandering through the palace as if
it really was her home. As if she had every right to
go where she pleased. She swept past the guards at
the entrance to Malak's rooms, and realized as she
inclined her head in their direction that she was perhaps more of a queen than she'd ever given herself
credit for.

Because they certainly treated her as if she had
every right to march straight past them.

Malak wasn't in his private dining room, and that
meant Shona had to explore the rest of the sprawl-
ing monarch's suite that she'd really only seen in
passing—too busy had she been with her gaze on
Malak. It was even more luxurious here, one room
leading into the next in a cascade of evident wealth.
She moved through all of them, paying little attention to the gilt and the gold, the huge paintings and
the towering statues, the marble floors covered in
rugs so soft and so delicate they felt like clouds.

And then, finally, she found him.

He was standing in what looked like a little art
gallery, the walls covered with portraits of stern men.

It took her a moment to realize that he looked like
all of the men in those portraits.

Shona didn't linger in the doorway. She didn't
wait for him to notice her or invite her in. Or worse,
bar her from entry. She marched straight in, then
headed across the gleaming black marble floor toward him.

Head high and chin tilted, as if she had every right.

"I cannot think of a single reason that you should be here." Malak did not turn and look at her. He kept his gaze trained on the portrait before him, of a man it took Shona longer than it should have to realize was his father.

He didn't have to look at her to hurt her, she discovered. He spoke in that same hard, dismissive voice that had made her bleed earlier, and that accomplished the same thing.

But the world had changed. *She* had changed. Whichever it was, she didn't believe him anymore. She didn't believe the things that had happened between them were some kind of game he had played. Honey instead of vinegar. Something deliberate and fake to sweeten the acquisition of his only heir.

The only way she could believe that was if she also believed that she was the piece of Louisiana trash she'd spent her life thinking she was. And maybe some part of her would always think that might be true. But the rest of her adamantly did not.

And if she was going to teach her son how to stand up not only for himself, but also for the people who would one day be his to lead, she needed to stand up for herself first.

Right here, right now.

No matter what it cost her. Because whatever the price was, it was better than cowering in an empty room somewhere and believing all the lies people had told her.

Shona was done with that. She was ready for what came next.

And that started with this man who had turned her life upside down—twice.

"I can think of any number of reasons for me to be here," she replied, her voice cool and even and a weapon all its own. She was proud of herself for that. "But first and foremost, Malak, I love you. Despite the fact you're being an ass."

CHAPTER THIRTEEN

THAT NO ONE else had ever dared call the great Sheikh Malak, the king of Khalia, an ass—to his face, at any rate—was immediately obvious.

The look he gave Shona was nothing short of amazed. Arrogant and astonished at once, and as he scowled at her he seemed like a thundercloud, filling the whole of the gallery without having to move a muscle.

But Shona had grown up in hurricanes. She only smiled at him. Serenely.

"Have you lost your mind entirely?" The question was quiet. Soft, even. But she didn't mistake it for any kind of weakness. Not when she could see that wild gleam in his dark green gaze. "Is this your version of a suicide mission, Shona?"

"I don't believe you," she told him, instead of answering his questions. "I don't believe a single thing you said to me earlier. I don't think you believe it, either."

"This is the trouble with innocence," Malak said, and there was a certain drawling disparagement in his tone that slid down her back like shame. But she straightened, because she understood on some level that shame was exactly what he wanted her to feel.

Which meant she refused. "I'm hardly an innocent."

"Not now, I grant you. But for all intents and purposes, you might as well have been a virgin. And I don't how to tell you this nicely, Shona, but what you are feeling is remarkably common."

"If that's your attempt to be nice, it failed."

He looked as if he pitied her, but she refused to give in to that scared part of her that urged her to slink away and lick her wounds somewhere else. Somewhere safe.

"This is what virgins do," Malak told her in that same tone. "They confuse sensation for emotion."

"I think what you mean to say is that this is what kings do," she replied, not backing down an inch, because this was the most important fight of her life. "Kings of this kingdom, anyway. In the face of any emotion they panic, don't they? Love is too big. Too unwieldy. It seems your father and your brother felt they had to choose between love and the throne."

"You know nothing about my father or my brother. And I would advise you to pick your words very carefully."

"You insisted that I take lessons, and I have. I imagine I know more about the recent history of this country than you do, because you lived it. You were in the thick of it. I've been studying the bigger picture." She reached out a hand and poked her finger into his chest, and realized after she'd done it that it had been entirely for the jagged sort of joy that exploded inside of her when she saw his expression. That intense *astonishment*, as if he couldn't believe a peasant had dared lay a hand on the king. But Shona dared. She dared everything. Because this was all or nothing and she'd spent her whole life with nothing already. She wanted *all*, for a change. She wanted Malak. "You have something neither your father nor your brother had."

"I know I do. I have their example and absolutely no desire to repeat their mistakes."

"No, Malak," Shona said softly, and she felt a kind of power wash through her. Power and certainty, washing her from her head down to her feet, as if she had always been a queen. As if she had always been meant to stand in a palace and claim her king. She held his gaze, her own serious and sure. "You have me."

Malak had never wanted anything more than he wanted Shona. Particularly right now.

But he could not allow himself such weakness.

"I have promised that I will marry you, if that is

what you mean—" he began, his tongue thick in his mouth. His throat too tight.

But this was not the woman he had left behind earlier, staring back at him in shock and hurt. This was the woman who had stared him down in a shoddy restaurant in the French Quarter as if he'd breached the walls of her private castle. This was the woman who had wanted nothing at all to do with him, even when he'd made it clear how much better he could make her life.

This was his Shona. His queen.

But he couldn't let that confuse the issue.

"I think you know that's not what I mean at all," she was saying in that same way of hers, as if her voice deserved to ring out over the whole of the desert the way it rang in him. "Do you think I don't understand what it's like to be afraid to love, Malak?"

It was as if she was strangling him when all she had done was poke a finger into the center of his chest. Her hands were nowhere near his throat, and even if they had been wrapped around it, he doubted very much she could have done him any harm.

And still he felt as if she was choking him.

"I do not fear love," he bit out, though the words felt bitter in his mouth. "I do not fear anything. Ask around. I am well known to be shockingly reckless in the face of any and all danger."

"You're talking about a different Malak," Shona said, with that certainty and dismissiveness that felt

like tectonic plates shifting deep inside him. "But
he died the day your brother abdicated the throne,
didn't he? The moment you had responsibilities, he
changed, because he had no choice. He rose to the
occasion. I know about that, too."

"Of course you do." His voice was acid. "Because
you ascended which throne, again?"

"Because I had a baby." Her voice was quiet. Mat-
ter-of-fact.

And pierced him straight through.

She held his gaze in that way of hers that made
it impossible to know if he should gather her close
or make absolutely certain that this time, when he
pushed her away, she stayed away.

But he couldn't seem to move.

And Shona continued. "I was twenty-two years
old and more alone than I think you can imagine.
And suddenly I was a mother. Whatever I felt,
whatever I thought my life was going to look like, it
changed in that moment. And part of that change was
daunting, sure. But sometimes I think it saved me."

He needed to say something—anything—to make
her stop before those tectonic plates inside him crum-
bled into dust, but she didn't seem to hear him.

"After all, when every single choice you make
has to be the responsible one because lives are at
stake, it almost feels like freedom, doesn't it? Because there's no room for error." That smile of hers
sliced him straight to the bone. It was sad and wise

and entirely too beautiful. Shona. "There's absolutely no way that you can do anything but the right thing, so that's what you do."

Malak was in agony. He didn't know what he wanted—or he wanted too much and all at once. He wanted to put his hands on her, but then he always did. He wanted to stop her talking, by any means necessary, but somehow he couldn't bring himself to do such a thing.

It was as if he was frozen solid yet lit on fire.

And worst of all, she seemed to know it.

"And I get that your parents were distant," she was saying, as if she was trying her best to tear him apart, here in this gallery filled with all the men whose shoes he doubted he could ever fill, staring down at him in disapproval. "Maybe they were even actively cruel. And I'm sympathetic. I am. But of all the women in all the world you could have chosen to have your baby, Malak, you picked the one who had even less in the way of parents than you did. At least you met your mother."

"My mother…" He hadn't meant to say that. It burst from his lips of its own accord and he wanted to hate her for that—but there was something in Shona's melting brown eyes. Something a whole lot like compassion, and it humbled him. "She hated me."

And all his life, when he said such things—always as a joke, an aside, a bit of a laugh—the people he'd said them to had denied it. Over and over again. "Of course she doesn't hate you," they would say. "Her emotions might be very complicated," they would assure him. "No mother hates her own child," they would say—but Malak had always thought they were making themselves feel better, not him.

Because he knew the truth now. His mother had wanted Adir. Malak was the consolation prize—and she'd hated him for it.

Shona didn't say any of those things. She didn't offer him anything even resembling a platitude. She only gazed at him for a moment, a knowledge in that gaze of hers that he didn't want to see.

"Maybe she did," she said quietly, and still, he was surprised the walls didn't shake with the force of it. "But that says a lot more about her than it ever could about you."

And something about that nearly snapped him in two.

"Shona—"

"I know all about it," she told him, and her eyes filled while she said it. It was almost more than he could bear. "Oh, God, do I know about it. And I've lived my whole life until now in response to every single thing they did to me when I was a kid. Or didn't do. The neglect. The cruelty. I could react to it forever. So could you. But where does it end?"

"Shona."

But still she didn't stop. Instead, she moved closer, that finger softening until her whole hand was on his chest. And he couldn't seem to set her away from him the way he knew he should.

The way he told himself he would any minute. Any minute now.

"I promised myself that I would never, ever allow Miles to feel even a moment of the kind of crap I lived through," Shona told him, fierce and solemn at once, and all that emotion turning her brown eyes brilliant. "And I won't. Don't you get it? We get to decide what his life is like. We get to decide what kind of man he becomes. Do you really want him to be like us, Malak? Do you want to break him before he even starts?"

There were tears on her cheeks. And equally as astonishing, his hands were on her shoulders, holding her.

He couldn't pretend he wasn't holding her.

"Never," he gritted out.

As if it was the most sacred vow he would ever utter.

"I have to believe that love is only as scary as we make it," Shona whispered. "I have to believe that we are not doomed to play out these same tired cycles over and over and over again. He deserves better, Malak." She reached up then, and fit her hand to his jaw, and in so doing knocked the world off its axis. "But so do we."

"I don't know how to do this," Malak managed to get out past the constriction in his throat, his chest.

He dipped his head so his face was next to hers. Close enough to kiss her—and yet he didn't. He couldn't, not just then. Not with the world in the balance between them. "I don't know how to do any of this. I don't know how to feel these things or—"

"I don't think you're supposed to know. I don't think anybody does."

"I have to be a king, Shona. I cannot be…this."

That last word came out raw. As if it was ripped from deep inside him. As if it was a rib he'd torn from his own chest.

And then it was as if the dam broke. He could no more keep the words inside than he could take his hands off her or step away. And he tried. He tried but failed to do anything but keep her close.

"I think of nothing but you," he told her, and he didn't know if he shouted or whispered. He couldn't hear a thing past the roaring in his ears. "You haunt my dreams. You're in my head wherever I go. This is madness."

He expected her to step away then; to fight him, because that was what she did. That was what *they* did.

But instead, incredibly, she smiled.

And it felt like sunlight, there in the middle of a dark desert night.

"It's not madness," Shona told him. "It's love."

"Love is not this red, fanged thing," he growled

at her. "Love is not dirty and wild and ravenous. It cannot be this full, this comprehensive, this—"

"This perfect?" she asked, still smiling. Shona shifted then, pushing herself up on her toes and balancing herself against his chest, her face tipped to his. "I hate to break it to you, my favorite little king, but all of that—all of this—is love."

He felt as if something roared in him then, something animal and intense. On some level, he was astounded that the walls of the castle didn't crumble where they stood, but they stayed tall and strong, and so did Shona, gazing back at him with water on her face and trust in her gaze.

Malak wanted nothing more than to earn that trust, no matter if it took him the rest of his life.

"I don't know why you think this could possibly work," he said, but he was gathering her close, as if his body knew things he was afraid to look at directly. "When all that has ever happened here is disaster."

"Because it has to work. Because there is no alternative."

Shona's smile went wicked, but it was the most beautiful thing Malak had ever seen. It lodged deep in his heart, where, he understood at last, she had been since the day he'd seen her draped in gold in a hotel bar so long ago.

Where she would always be, for the rest of their lives.

"Haven't you heard?" she asked, there against his mouth, fit tight against him as if she'd been made for him. Malak knew she had. "I am always right. After all, I am the queen of Khalia."

CHAPTER FOURTEEN

IT WAS THE grandest wedding in Khalian history.

Or so Shona was told at every turn.

It took days. It followed typical Arabic custom, and Shona found that she loved every part of that except the traditional separation of bride and groom. By the time they got to the actual wedding ceremony, and the reception that seemed to include every last person in the kingdom as well as the entire world, she thought she might fall to pieces if she didn't get some time alone with Malak.

In bed and out.

But queens did not necessarily get what they wanted, or not instantly anyway, she discovered. She had to greet a thousand people. She had to smile and nod and talk about the orphan initiatives she was putting into play after the wedding, because she'd taken what Malak had said about the good she could do seriously. She had to remember the names of every important person who appeared before her and clearly knew hers, and found to her dismay that she had to draw on every last one of the comportment classes she had tried so hard to avoid.

She met neighboring kings. She met Malak's brother and sister. Zufar, the man who had given up the throne, and the wife who clearly made him so happy, making it obvious he'd made the right choice. Galila, who greeted Shona as if they were already friends, which eased a kind of tension inside Shona that she hadn't known she was holding onto.

It was as if they were already a family, Shona thought at one point, and she was a part of it.

Family. It was something she'd never had before. Not really. It was something she'd never believed in.

And it seemed to be the order of the day, she thought, when her brand-new husband and his brother and sister were all smiles, built bridges and olive branches, with their imposing half brother, Adir.

Even the old king made an effort, mustering up one of his rare smiles and wearing it throughout the reception, as he greeted all the people he no longer ruled. But the best part, as far as Shona was concerned, was when he took Malak's hands, called him his son and his king in the next breath, then turned to Shona and welcomed her like a daughter.

More family. So much family Shona was tempted to believe in it despite herself.

Miles, of course, was beside himself with joy. The crown prince of the kingdom smiled and laughed and told anybody who would listen that his parents were married at last and they really were a family.

King, queen and crown prince together, at last.

It all made Shona giddy.

And this time, if the other shoe dared try to fall on her, she planned to burn it in midair.

Because the queen of Khalia wanted to believe in happy families and love, thank you. Not ugly old shoes.

Finally, it was time for the bride and groom to leave.

Malak took her hands and led her from the reception that sprawled over the entire first floor of the palace, which had been thrown wide open to let in as many members of the public as could fit, all wild with joy for their new king and this next chapter for their kingdom.

"This does not look like the way to your bedroom," Shona told him when he led her outside.

"I am afraid you will have to wait, little one," Malak replied, grinning. And then he led her across the wide courtyard to where a gleaming black helicopter sat waiting. He helped her on board, and soon enough they were aloft.

The pilot flew them up and over the capital city, with all its towers and bells ringing out the kingdom's joy at their union. They continued out over the desert, until all there was in every direction were the rolling, brooding sands. And for a long time, there was nothing below them but the ripple of the desert, the odd tide, stretching out toward the horizon.

The helicopter began its descent, and it was only as it lowered that Shona saw where they were headed. A splotch of impossible green in the middle of all that sand. She caught her breath, because she knew what this place was—what it had to be—and it was even more magical than she could have imagined.

"Welcome to my oasis," Malak said when he helped her out of the helicopter. "I regret I cannot give you a fairy tale. But I can give you this."

"It's perfect." She smiled at him, her heart too big for her chest. "It's all perfect."

There were pools of sparkling water ringed by date trees. Palms rustled overhead, and bright tents waited on the far side of the pools, with stout walls of fabric to keep out the sand.

But in the middle of everything was Malak. And he was all that mattered. They could have been back in her falling down old house in New Orleans and she would have felt just like this.

Brighter than anyone should be without bursting into flame.

"I love you," Malak told her when he led her into the biggest tent, which was furnished like an apartment—but like no apartment Shona had ever seen. A four-poster bed rose to one side, a living area complete with couches and pillows to the other, while thick rugs made it seem as if they weren't in the middle of a desert at all.

Malak drew her to him and gazed down at her, and Shona forgot the luxuriousness of their surroundings—because there was nothing but him. Nothing but them.

"I love you, Shona," her husband, her king, the love of her life, told her. "You gave me my son. And then you gave me the world. And in return, I will give you everything I have. And all that I am."

"I appreciate that," she murmured, and laughed when his eyebrows rose in that expression of arrogant astonishment that she loved perhaps more than she should have. "But I suspect my wedding gift is better."

"Better than the love and devotion of the king of Khalia? The mind boggles."

Shona reached out and took his hands in hers, then drew them to the slope of her belly, and held them there.

Awareness and a kind of awe dawned on Malak's face, his hands tightened against her belly, and Shona smiled in the vain hope that it might keep the tears at bay.

It didn't. And she couldn't say she cared.

"The palace doctor tells me I'm nearly six weeks along," she whispered.

"Shona…" he whispered, as if she was the miracle. Not the life they had sparked inside of her.

"I love you, too," she told him, with all that she was. "And we will love these babies of ours. And you will not only be a marvelous king, Malak. You'll be the best father. I know it."

"If I'm any kind of father at all, it is because of you."

And then he was lifting her up, holding her above him and then letting her slide down into his kiss. He wrapped his arms around her and he held her there, for what seemed like forever.

"You already gave me Miles," he said, his voice thick with emotion, and for once her brave and proud Malak made no attempt to hide it. "And you give me you, every day and every night. I know I can't possibly deserve any part of this. Any part of you."

Shona reached out and ran her hand over his jaw, then slid it around the back of his neck.

"It's not about deserving it. It's about doing it." She kissed him then. Sweetly, but with the promise of all that heat that only seemed to grow between them. "All we have to do is believe we can."

"I believe it," Malak said fiercely.

And he carried her to that four-poster bed, lay down with her in the middle of a forbidden desert oasis that was like something out of a dream and they started on their forever.

One perfect kiss at a time.

* * * * *

If you enjoyed
Sheikh's Secret Love-Child
by Caitlin Crews
look out for the rest of the
Bound to the Desert King series!

Sheikh's Baby of Revenge
by Tara Pammi
Sheikh's Pregnant Cinderella
by Maya Blake
Sheikh's Princess of Convenience
by Dani Collins

Available now!

#3677 AN INNOCENT, A SEDUCTION, A SECRET
One Night With Consequences
by Abby Green
When Seb spies Edie's talent for lavish interior decoration, he makes an irresistible job offer—spend the festive season decorating his opulent home! But soon, Edie becomes the sensual gift Seb wishes to unwrap...

#3678 THE BILLIONAIRE'S CHRISTMAS CINDERELLA
by Carol Marinelli
Abe Devereux is famed for his cold heart. So meeting Naomi, who's determined to see the good in him, is a novelty. But will seducing her be his biggest risk, or his greatest chance of redemption?

#3679 PREGNANT BY THE DESERT KING
by Susan Stephens
Lucy is shocked by Tadj's royal revelation: Lucy is carrying the baby of a desert king! Tadj will secure his heir, but can Lucy accept his scandalous solution—that she share his royal bed?

#3680 THE VIRGIN'S SICILIAN PROTECTOR
by Chantelle Shaw
Hired to keep heiress Ariana safe, wealthy bodyguard Santino is intrigued by her hidden vulnerability. Their sexual tension is electric! And when Santino discovers just how innocent Ariana is, resisting her temptation becomes an impossible challenge...

Get 4 FREE REWARDS!

We'll send you 2 FREE Books
plus 2 FREE Mystery Gifts.

YES! Please send me 2 FREE Harlequin Presents® novels and my 2 FREE gifts (gifts are worth about $10 retail). After receiving them, if I don't wish to receive any more books, I can return the shipping statement marked "cancel." If I don't cancel, I will receive 6 brand-new novels every month and be billed just $4.55 each for the regular-print edition or $5.55 each for the larger-print edition in the U.S., or $5.49 each for the regular-print edition or $5.99 each for the larger-print edition in Canada. That's a savings of at least 11% off the cover price! It's quite a bargain! Shipping and handling is just 50¢ per book in the U.S. and 75¢ per book in Canada*. I understand that accepting the 2 free books and gifts places me under no obligation to buy anything. I can always return a shipment and cancel at any time. The free books and gifts are mine to keep no matter what I decide.

Choose one: ☐ **Harlequin Presents®**
Regular-Print
(106/306 HDN GMYX)

☐ **Harlequin Presents®**
Larger-Print
(176/376 HDN GMYX)

Name (please print)

Address   Apt. #

City   State/Province   Zip/Postal Code

Mail to the **Reader Service**:
IN U.S.A.: P.O. Box 1341, Buffalo, NY 14240-8531
IN CANADA: P.O. Box 603, Fort Erie, Ontario L2A 5X3

Want to try two free books from another series? Call 1-800-873-8635 or visit www.ReaderService.com.

HP17

He set his glass down with a clatter. "I am his *father.* I
have missed three years of his life. You think a *weekend
pass* is going to suffice? A few dips in the Caribbean as he
learns to swim?" He fixed his gaze on hers. "I want *every
day* with him. I want it *all.*"

"What else can we do?" she queried helplessly. "You
live in New York and I live here. Leo is settled and
happy. A limited custody arrangement is the only realistic
proposition."

"It is *not* a viable proposition." His low growl made
her jump. "That's not going to work, Gia."

She eyed him warily. "Which part?"

"All of it." He waved a Rolex-clad wrist at her. "I
have a proposal for you. It's the only one on the table,
nonnegotiable on all points. Take it or leave it."

The wariness written across her face intensified. "Which is?"

"We do what's in the best interests of our child. You marry me, we create a life together in New York and give Leo the family he deserves."

Don't miss
Married for a One-Night Consequence,
available December 2018 wherever
Harlequin Presents® books and ebooks are sold.

www.Harlequin.com

HARLEQUIN *Presents*

Coming next month—a festive trio just in time
for the holidays!

Claiming His Christmas Wife by Dani Collins

Part of the Conveniently Wed! miniseries

When Imogen faints in the cold New York snow,
Travis is called to his ex-wife's very public rescue!
But, with a deal *just* for Christmas, will he be able
to let Imogen go a second time?

Bound by Their Christmas Baby by Clare Connelly

Part of the Christmas Seductions miniseries

When brooding bachelor Gabe learns Abby is his business
rival's daughter, he's furious. So what will he do when she
returns the following Christmas with their secret baby?

The Billionaire's Christmas Cinderella by Carol Marinelli

Tycoon Abe is overwhelmed by the potency of his
undeniable connection with Naomi. Now he wants
this shy Cinderella between his sheets by Christmas!

Available December 2018